USA TODAY BESTSELLING AUTHOR
ERIN BEDFORD

UNTIL
MIDNIGHT

Also by Erin Bedford

The Underground Series
Chasing Rabbits
Chasing Cats
Chasing Princes
Chasing Shadows
Chasing Hearts
The Crimes of Alice
Hatter's Heart

The Mary Wiles Chronicles
Marked by Hell
Bound by Hell
Deceived by Hell
Tempted by Hell

Starcrossed Dragons
Riding Lightning
Grinding Frost
Swallowing Fire
Pounding Earth

The Crimson Fold
Until Midnight
Until Dawn
Until Sunset

Curse of the Fairy Tales
Rapunzel Untamed
Rapunzel Unveiled

Rapunzel Unchained

Her Angels
Heaven's Embrace
Heaven's A Beach
Heaven's Most Wanted

House of Durand
Indebted to the Vampires
Wanted by the Vampires
Protected by the Vampires
Embrace of the Vampires
Tempted by the Butler
Loved by the Vampires
Huntress of the Vampires

Academy of Witches
Witching On A Star
As You Witch
Witch You Were Here
Just Witch It
Summer Witchin'

Children of the Fallen
Death In Her Eyes
Fire In Her Blood

The Beast of the Fae Court
Granting Her Wish
Vampire CEO

ERIN BEDFORD

UNTIL MIDNIGHT

Chapter 1

THE HOUSE WAS SILENT as I crept from my bed. No one else would wake until well after ten. By then I would be long gone.

I slipped into my clothes, a pair of fitted black pants and a tan shirt with laces at the neckline. My boots I carried so they wouldn't give me away as I made my way through the house.

Back home I wouldn't have had to sneak out. My father and I would have both been awake by now, and ready to start the day, but he wasn't here, and this wasn't home. Not really.

Stopping by the kitchen, I grabbed an apple from the bowl on the table. Missy, a plump older woman, ran the kitchen and would have been cross with me for eating before the designated meal time. I was still in disbelief we even had a cook, let alone the fact she didn't usually wake until eight-thirty.

The rest of the Inner Circle, or the Soft Hands as we liked to call them back home in the Glade, weren't much different. The paved streets were quiet with only one or two early risers walking about like me. Back in the Glade, the streets were barely able to be called that, mainly made of dirt and scattered rock. I'd become so accustomed to those hard trails that making the trek through the town now felt like floating on a cloud.

I ate my apple as I headed for my usual place, the juices almost too sweet for my taste buds. Even the food tasted different here. Bland meals with too ripe fruit filled our table in the Glades. Despite my father being head of the farm faction, we didn't eat much different from the rest of the workers.

The first time I had eaten with our new family I had become violently ill. I'd only been able to eat small amounts of food until my stomach became used to it. My taste buds still hadn't adjusted, nor myself in general.

When I finally passed the last of the two-storied houses, something else I had to get used to compared to our hovel in the Glade, I sighed. All my built-up tension seemed to float out of me as I scanned the open field. There weren't many places like this in the Inner Circle. Most of the space had been utilized for one reason or another.

"We must be useful, Clarabelle," my stepmother had made a habit of telling me.

"Useful." I snorted to myself as I strolled into the open area. Houses packed together side by side, barely enough room to walk let alone breathe? It didn't seem very useful to me.

But here, out in the open air without the hustle and bustle of their busy streets, I found my solace. This place was useful. If for no other reason than my sanity.

I sat down on the grass. Even these green blades, like the rest of the town, had a fake shine to it. When the sun hit it just right, the field shone like emeralds, something that could only been manufactured. A poor substitute for the fields back home.

Letting out a deep breath, I lay back on the ground not caring that the grass would get stuck in my dark hair. My stepmother would have a cow if she saw me. Just one more thing to add to the list of grievances against me.

Why she had married my father bewildered me. They were nothing alike. While she held a cool disregard for anyone other than her precious daughters, mini versions of herself, my father loved all living creatures and never found a person he didn't like or who didn't like him in return. So, when he came home one day from delivering the weekly crops to announce he'd married, I'd been more than a little surprised by his choice.

My mother, Savior rest her soul, had died not four winters before and while I hadn't expected my father to stay a widower forever, I had at least expected him to pick someone from the Glade. Someone who knew what life was like there, the hardships and the good. Belinda Seam wouldn't know hard work if it bit her in her perfectly fluffed behind.

I finished my apple, tossed the core into the field, and then went and picked it up. It wouldn't disintegrate back into the earth, like in the Glade; the ground here held too much metal and rock in it to do it any good.

So, I tucked the remains of my apple into my pocket and headed back to town. The time I had spent in the little field had been long enough for the market to open. There weren't many buyers at this time of the day but enough that many of the shops would lazily show their wares.

Finding a trash receptacle, I dropped in my apple core. Its contents would be shipped off to Middleton, the industrial part of the bands which circled the Core. It sat between the Inner Circle and the Glade. I'd never been there, but I'd been told they had it even worse than us on the outskirts. Most of the jobs were underground, leaving the people covered in dirt and their eyes sensitive to the sun. It was what got them the nickname 'Moles', though I doubted they would have appreciated it.

"Hey, Clarabelle," Marsha called out from the meat stand. When the tall, beefy guy had told me his name was Marsha it had taken everything within me not to giggle. Men just weren't named that in the Glade. But like so many differences between our two worlds, names were only the tip of the iceberg.

"Please, Clara." I winced at my full name. "Clarabelle always makes me feel like you're calling a cow."

"Sorry." Marsha chuckled making his pale blue eyes crinkle at the sides. "I see you are up early as always. Don't you ever sleep?"

"Force of habit," I replied, casting my eyes down on the slabs of meat before me. Beef, fish, and a large selection of poultry were neatly displayed with little tags. So many choices for such a small population. We didn't have such a selection back home. Sometimes we were lucky to have meat at all. Most of the food ended up shipped here or to the Core, leaving the workers with just enough to survive.

Anger filled me at the sight of it all. The system made no sense to me, but whenever anyone questioned it, we were told it was just the way it was and to be happy with what we had. Well, I had been until I'd moved here and saw how much better they lived compared to us. Now I had sudden spouts of rage at how blind we had been to the injustice in our lives and how powerless I was to stop it.

"Are you excited?" Marsha asked jerking me out of my internal fight. My gaze met his expectant one and my brow furrowed. Seeing my confusion, he added, "You know about today?"

"What about today?"

He laughed; a sort of hard noise that ended abruptly. "I thought all the girls counted down until Election day."

The term held some familiarity, but I couldn't quite place it. I knew we had learned something like that in class before we went to work in the fields, but I couldn't remember what it was about.

Not wanting to look like even more than an idiot, I shrugged. "Not this girl."

"Oh, really?" He chuckled before holding up a finger as a customer approached. Marsha wrapped up a few packages of beef and veal. As he handed it to the young woman, he gave her a wink. He always had the girls blushing, old or young, it didn't matter. His charms only went so far with me though. Even as a butcher he was too clean, too much like them.

"Yes, really," I responded once she had left. "I don't care about that kind of thing."

"Not even for the chance to meet them?" Marsha lowered his voice to a mysterious timbre.

"You mean, the Core?" I glanced away from his stall toward the large castle that loomed over the Inner Circle. From the Glade, we could barely make out its peaks, but from here it shadowed the town by early afternoon.

"No," Marsha murmured. "The Crimson Fold."

I turned back to him in a rush, my mouth forming the shape of an o. The Crimson Fold, the elites who lived in the Core, never came down from their palace. We only knew they existed because of the decrees they sent out every few years or so. They were always marked with a blood-red wax seal and the signature, 'The Crimson Fold'.

Why they wanted to name themselves something so image-provoking confused many. But since they were silent rulers who didn't give us too much grief, most people didn't think much of it. I know I hadn't until now.

"I suppose it would be nice to finally meet the face behind the paper." I smirked at

Marsha who gave me a weird smile in return.

"Well, I wouldn't worry too much about it in your case." He turned away from me to pick up more wrapping paper. "You have a fifty-fifty chance of being chosen anyhow."

"Why's that?" I cocked a brow, his sudden change in demeanor unsettling.

"Your sister is of age, isn't she?"

"Stepsister," I corrected and then wished I hadn't. The more people who knew of my displeasure of being part of their family, the more grief my stepmother would give me. "I mean, Julianna just turned seventeen."

"Then she's more likely to be picked than you." He offered me a wink before adding. "Then you and Lea should be set for the future. Could you imagine?" Marsha stared up at the sky, a dreamy look covering his face. "Being rich enough to do whatever you want to do for the rest of your life."

"I don't. My family seems rich enough as it is now," I muttered, unable to keep the bitterness out of my voice. As far as I knew, we had more than enough to live off for years to come. Who needed much more than that?

"Either way," Marsha continued looking back down to his work, "with you and Julianna being of age little Lea won't have to worry about anything."

Very soon, the market began to get busy, and Marsha couldn't stand there any longer to talk to me. I waved goodbye and started my own shopping.

As I stopped at different stalls, some for food, others for frivolous trinkets, my mind whirled. Lea, my younger stepsister, had only hit fourteen not too many weeks ago, but in my opinion, she still acted like a toddler. Living in the Inner Circle, she wouldn't have to worry about anything until she went to find a spouse, and even then, she'd have her pick.

My stepmother might not get her hands dirty, but she could sew a dress like no other and had a waiting list a mile long for her creations. It was that list that kept her so lofty in her perch. I had my fair share of congratulations for my father's good fortune. It seemed more like a curse to me, but since I didn't have much of a choice in the matter, my thoughts weren't important. Like most things, it seemed.

Marsha's talk of the Election had me paying more attention to the people around me. Especially the girls. They all went about their day as normal, but there seemed to be an underlying excitement. Whispers here and there that to any other person would look like friends exchanging secrets, but from the way their eyes repeatedly went to the Core, I could guess what they were talking about.

When I arrived home, the quiet of the house had transformed into mayhem. My stepmother and siblings argued in the living room. They were almost identical with their pale hair and dark brown eyes, their voices the same nasal pitch. Their words overlapped too much for me to make out what they were arguing about. Probably something about the latest fashions, no doubt.

I sat my purchases from the market down on the side table, the contents making a noise as they found purchase in their spot. The sound must have alerted my step-family to my presence because their arguing promptly stopped. I turned slowly from the table to find three pairs of eyes on me. Each of them filled with a different emotion.

Lea's eyes held amusement as if what they fought about had no real importance, while Julianna's couldn't be livider. She hadn't liked me much before, but now for some reason or another, I had gotten on her bad side. Not that she had much of a good side to begin with.

My stepmother's expression held a mixture of emotions. Frustration, irritation, and possibly relief? An odd combination; I didn't know what to make of it. Or any of them for that matter.

"What's going on?" I asked finally, stepping toward the trio.

Julianna's hands tightened into fists as she stomped toward me with a finger pointed at my chest, she snarled, "I'll tell you what's going on. You have ruined my life!"

I frowned. I'd ruined her life? I doubted that. I'd done as much as I could to be as little in her life as possible. The only time I really participated in our little family was at mandatory family dinners, and even those were rare.

"I'm sorry, I'm not sure what you are talking about." I held my hands open to my sides, looking to the others for some enlightenment.

Lea giggled but when her mother shot her a warning look, she clapped her hands over her mouth stifling the sound.

My attention turned to my stepmother who seemed to know exactly what I had done to cause such an uproar. The emotion on her face disappeared as a mask of indifference, one I had seen too often sent my way, took its place. Approaching me, she held out something.

A bright red envelope sat in her hand. My brow furrowed in confusion as I took it from her. The back of it bore the dark red wax seal of the Core, the Crimson Fold. Just from the seal alone, I knew what I held in my hand, why my stepsister and stepmother were so upset.

This envelope held an invitation to the ball. The event Marsha had told me about. The one every girl in the Inner Circle was anxiously awaiting an invitation to. And here we had one, but with one problem.

It had my name on it.

Chapter 2

AS THE OVERSEER'S DAUGHTER, I didn't get invited to many gatherings. Most of the other kids my age were too worried I'd rat them out for one reason or another.

The first and only time I had received an invitation had been on my twelfth summer. The same mixture of excitement and dread I had felt then, now swirled in my stomach as I held the blood-red paper in my hand.

"So, what does this mean?" I met my stepmother's gaze as my brow furrowed. I ignored the withering glare Julianna shot my way, preferring the least of the three evils.

Belinda snatched the envelope out of my hand and waved it in the air with a rough laugh. "You don't even know what you hold in your hand, you silly girl."

Crossing my arms over my chest, I huffed. "Then why don't you enlighten me? I'm assuming it has something to do with this Election I've heard so little about?"

My stepmother's forehead crinkled showing her age, something she would be appalled to know had she seen it. "Who have you been talking to? I thought those in the outer circles weren't included in the Election?" She glanced at her daughters before the accusation in her eyes fell on me.

"I've heard about it before, but not much," I admitted but not including Marsha in my story. If I wasn't supposed to know about it, then the more I knew, the better.

Julianna scoffed and rolled her eyes. "She doesn't deserve to be invited. She doesn't even know what she is being invited to, let alone what an honor it is." Julianna's eyes zeroed in on the envelope still in her mother's hands. "In fact, why don't I just take your place? They won't know the difference, no one even knows you." She tried to take the envelope from her mother's hands, but Belinda moved it out of her reach.

"Ah ah ah," Belinda shook her head. "You know it doesn't work that way. Even if Clarabelle" - she shot me a look of disdain - "isn't well-known, the envelope is bonded by blood. Remember what happened to Gemina?"

Julianna's eyes widened, and fear crossed her face before she turned away with a pout. I almost asked who Gemina was and what happened to her when Lea jumped in.

She grabbed my hands with a giggle. "Oh, Clarabelle, you are just going to love it. The dresses, the food ... oh," - she skipped in place, making me giggle myself - "and the ball! It'll be so much fun. I only wish I had been invited, but you know the youngest child never gets invited." Her lip curled out and her gaze dropped.

I sighed and ran a hand through my hair. "So, what exactly am I getting into? Just going to some party? I don't see how that's such a big deal."

The three looks of utter abhorrence came my way so suddenly, I had to take a step back. Maybe it was a bigger deal than I had thought.

"The big deal," Belinda snapped, "is that this could change our lives forever. Not only would you get to live a life of luxury high up in the capital for the rest of your days, but we" - she gestured around to the three of them - "will never have to work another day in our lives. Julianna and Lea will be able to marry," Lea made a disgusted noise, causing Belinda to add, "Or not. Whatever they want to do, and all from you going to one little party." She held the invitation out to me with an eager grin.

I took the envelope from her with a hesitant hand. Flipping it over in my hand, I gave her a small unsure smile before putting my fingers on the wax seal. I almost opened it but then stopped at a thought. "I really should wait until my father gets home and find out what he thinks of all this."

"No!" Belinda and Julianna shouted at the same time, but then Belinda glared at her daughter. Julianna's lips pressed tightly together, and she stared down at the floor. Belinda stepped toward and placed her hands on my shoulders.

"Look, your father won't be home until tomorrow, and this is a twenty-four-hour invitation. You can't just wait until he comes home. It'll be too late by then."

Her explanation made me frown. A twenty-four-hour window? What did the Crimson Fold have up their sleeves? The thought of going to this thing seemed more and more like a bad idea.

I pulled away from her grasp, turning my back to them. Marsha's words from earlier filled my head. He had said I had a fifty-fifty chance of being picked and I shouldn't worry. The way he had made it sound had been like being invited was a good thing, and even my stepfamily thought I should be happy about it. Julianna sure seemed pissed I'd gotten the invite over her, so why should I worry about being invited? And why had Belinda been so relieved for me to receive it instead of her daughter?

There were so many questions and yet no time to figure out what exactly I would be getting into. The smart thing would be to wait until my father arrived home. He would know what to do, and I trusted him not to lie to me. Not like Belinda might.

Turning back to their anxious faces, I said, "I'm going to wait for my father."

Lea and Julianna blew up, arguing over each other and then turning to their mother when I didn't respond in kind. Belinda though had become unusually calm, not blowing her top the way she usually did when I dragged mud onto the carpet.

She waved her daughters off, and they instantly quieted like the good little drones they were. Her gaze leveled on me with a careful expression as if she were afraid to show me too much. "I understand how you feel, Clarabelle."

"You do?" I cocked a brow, not believing her for a second.

"Of course, I do." She was trying to console me. It wasn't working. "You've been taken away from your home, put into a house you don't know with people you just met. You have no reason to trust us or our ways, but believe me when I tell you, this isn't something you want to trifle with. You don't want to anger them."

"Why?" I countered. "What would they do if I don't go?"

Before my stepmother could answer, Julianna rushed to my side and grabbed me by the arm. Her nails dug into my skin as she shrieked, "We'll be outcasts, that's what! Pariahs. Forget having a choice in spouses, we'd be lucky to have food on our table."

I pulled my arm away from her, forcing myself not to wince. She'd probably left marks from the sharp pincers she called nails. Turning away from Julianna, who tended to exaggerate, I looked to my stepmother. The glare of disapproval on her face gave me hope it wouldn't be as bad as Julianna had said.

"While not exactly the delivery I would have approved of," - Belinda pushed her eldest daughter behind her with a frown - "but my daughter is right."

Crap.

"If you don't go," she said calmly, "we won't only be shunned by the people, but we will be forced from our home, forced to move to another ring." Her nose wrinkled in disgust before she sighed. "Basically, our lives will be changed forever no matter your decision."

I had no pity for her or her daughters. They had been living in luxury here in the Inner Circle. Part of me wanted to be petty and say they deserved whatever they got, but I knew my father wouldn't like that. I remembered what he said to me when he told me we were moving to the Inner Circle.

"I want you to have everything I could never give you here, Clara." He'd cupped my face, giving me a smile.

"But I don't need anything else," I'd tried to argue with him, tears in my eyes. I hadn't understood why he'd thought he needed to uproot me from my home to live with strangers. Sure, I didn't have many friends in the Glade, but at least it was home, not like the cold house of my new step-family.

When I'd arrived in the Inner Circle, I'd realized what my father had meant. They had so much more than we would ever have. I'd never have to worry about going hungry again or having threadbare clothing. But I'd give it all up to go back home to our tiny house in the Glade. Where my mother had hung sunflower-printed curtains in the kitchen, and where she had died from pneumonia the following winter.

Thinking of my mother made me realize something. I didn't want my stepfamily to move to the Glade. To have them there, in the house in which my mother had lived, would be to taint everything I loved about it. Unfortunately, the only way to make sure that didn't happen was to accept the invitation and go to the ball.

"Fine," I sighed in defeat. "I'll go."

Lea and Julianna cheered and clapped their hands while their mother let out a relieved breath and then nodded toward the envelope. "Then you should open the invitation right away."

"Why does it matter if I open it now or not?" I stared back down at the object in question.

"Because once you open it, they will know you have accepted." I didn't like the mysterious tone of her voice; I didn't like mysteries. Things in life should be simple: you work, you eat, you die. Fancy envelopes with strange powers were not something I wanted in my life.

Already regretting my decision to go, I grasped the wax seal between my thumb and forefinger and pulled. Pain instantly radiated through my finger. I jerked it back quickly popping it into my mouth. Coppery blood filled my mouth and my gaze shot back to the seal. Inside it sat the tiny pin that had pricked my finger.

What kind of person would do such a thing? But then again, what kind of people invite a bunch of strangers to their home for a party with lethal consequences if you declined?

Self-important people, that's who.

Once my finger stopped bleeding, I reached into the envelope careful of any other surprises. Inside sat an off-white rectangle with curly blood-red writing on it.

Clarabelle Feldson,

You have been cordially invited to attend Alban's annual Election Ceremony. In the next 48 hours, transportation will be provided to bring you to the Core. There you shall be provided with every item you would possibly need until your place has been decided.

Thank you for your contribution to Alban.

It was signed 'The Crimson Fold' and stamped with a miniature version of their sign.

My heart raced as I realized what this meant. My father wouldn't be home in time to see me off. He wouldn't even know why I wasn't home unless Belinda told him, and I bet she knew this.

Rage swept through me, and I crumbled the invitation in my hand. "You knew about this, didn't you?" I pointed at my stepmother, my fingers still gripping the crushed paper.

"Whatever do you mean?" She placed her hand on her chest, an innocent expression on her face.

I didn't believe it for one second. "They'll be here to collect me before father ever gets home. So, I wouldn't have a chance to change my mind or even talk to him about it."

Belinda shrugged, not bothering to deny it. "We don't question their rules, just obey them. You'd know that if you had grown up here and not ... well, where you did."

"Well, I have news for you," I snarled. "I'm not going." I tossed the envelope and the destroyed invitation at her feet before stomping away.

As I marched up the stairs, Belinda called out to me, "It doesn't matter now, you've already accepted. They'll take you now, whether you want to go or not."

For some reason, her words didn't make me any madder than Marsha's his cryptic reassurances did. Fifty-fifty my butt.

Chapter 3

I DIDN'T LEAVE MY room for the rest of the evening. My anger filled my stomach allowing me to miss dinner without much of a thought.

Not like I hadn't gone to bed hungry before. Once, when the harvest hadn't been good my father and I had lived off broth for weeks, if it could have been called broth. It wasn't much more than water, a few chicken bones, and some herbs from the garden. Those nights I had been so hungry, I'd have eaten grass if I hadn't already known it would just make me throw up the little food I already had in my stomach.

It was all their fault. I sat on my bed and glared out the window at the semi-dark sky toward the looming building. My bedroom faced toward the Core so that I could see the castle in the center.

I'd never given them much thought before. The Crimson Fold, whoever they really were, didn't bother with us in the Glade. We only grew and harvested the food the whole of Alban ate. Nurtured and slaughtered the meat sent to each area, the majority of it to the Core, another portion to the Soft Hands, and an even smaller portion to the Moles. In the Glade, we were lucky to get whatever was left over.

One would think those creating the food would get most it, but no. We weren't important enough. Our lives didn't matter. Hell, we hadn't mattered enough to know about Election Day, other than a whisper here or there. They probably didn't want a worn-down barely fed contestant. Well, I had news for them.

A small smile touched my lips as I imagined what they would think when they realized they had invited the wrong daughter. Sure, I had filled out a bit since I'd moved to the Inner Circle, but a few months here wouldn't get rid of years' worth of working in the fields. My hands would never be soft and dainty. My skin would always be speckled with sunspots from hours out of the shade. No, I certainly didn't look like any of the sheltered children of the Inner Circle.

I didn't think like them either.

What would they do when they realized I wouldn't play along? I didn't know the right silverware to use or how to act at a fancy event. I'd only ever worn a dress once, and that had been at my mother's funeral. Even then it had only been for a few minutes before we had to go back to the fields. The crop didn't wait just because your mother died.

I'd been grateful then for the distraction. As I'd dug into the earth, I'd shoved all my hurt and anger into it. No child should have to bury their parent, and I didn't blame the sickness at the time. I blamed the Core. It had been their fault we hadn't had enough food half the time. They took and took and never gave us anything in return. If we'd lived in the Inner Circle, my mother, beautiful and kind, could have gotten the medicine she'd needed to survive.

The coppery taste of blood pulled me out of my thoughts, and I winced. In my anguish I had bitten into my cheek, a bad habit I had yet to figure out how to break.

Closing my eyes, I took a deep breath and counted very slowly down from ten. When I reached zero, I let out all the air and opened my eyes. The castle still stood there as if laughing haughtily at me, but I felt better. More stable.

I'd been tricked into this, but I wouldn't let it rule me. I'd go to their party and show them I wasn't someone to trifle with. And who knew? Maybe I'd get to meet our mysterious leader, Patrick Blordril, the third leader of Alban since its creation. Maybe he could tell me why people starve in the other rings while he and the Soft Hands had more than enough food to feed everyone twice over.

I lay down on my bed, tossing and turning to find a comfortable position. Pulling the pillow out from under my head, I flung it to the ground. Without the pillow, I could pretend the bed I slept in belonged back home, but even then, it felt like a trick. The bed, like the pillow, too soft to be from home.

Eventually, I fell into a restless slumber, my mind filled with blood, filled envelopes and laughing masked faces. They chased me down long corridors, wanting me to eat from trays of food covered with fingers and toes. I woke from the dream screaming while the sun beamed down on my face.

I jumped at the pounding at the door, and I scanned the room like a frightened rabbit. My heartbeat began to slow as I realized I wasn't dreaming anymore and that the banging sound was just someone knocking on the front door.

Slipping from the bed, I glanced at the clock. After eleven! I'd never slept so long in my life. Most of the day had already gone, and that meant the knocking at the door might mean they'd come to collect me.

I paused at my bedroom door, no longer wanting to answer it. Maybe if no one came to the door, they would turn around and leave without me? As I thought it, I knew it was a foolish wish. Even more so when Missy answered the door with her usual cheer, "'Ello!"

The muffled voice responding to her sounded familiar, but I couldn't place it. My hand went to my doorknob, and as I was about to twist the lock into place, Missy called out, "Clarabelle, the butcher boy is here to see you!"

The butcher boy?

Instead of locking the door, I opened it and raced to the edge of the stairs. There stood Marsha, a grim expression on his face. When he saw me coming down the stairs, it didn't lighten much either.

"Marsha," I said as I landed before him. "What are you doing here?"

He didn't answer at first, his hands twisting in his apron. He was still dressed in the white shirt and tan pants he normally wore to work, his apron tied over it. Blood spatter colored the pristine white material, and my mind instantly went to yesterday's invitation.

"You heard, didn't you?" I asked, not elaborating more than that. Why else would he show up on my doorstep unannounced?

"I'm so sorry, Clara." He ran a hand through his hair and sighed. He truly seemed in anguish from the whole thing.

"It's not your fault." I shook my head, not sure why he was apologizing. "You couldn't have known I would be the one."

"But I'm the one who said you wouldn't be picked." He stamped his foot in frustration, and his shoe left a scuff on the tile, earning him a glare from Missy. "If I hadn't said anything about it, then you wouldn't have been chosen, and it would be Julianna who would be going to this thing and not you."

I sent Missy a look, asking her to give me a minute. The older woman gave me a displeased frown before stomping away toward the kitchen. When she was gone and out of earshot, I moved closer to Marsha.

"Hey," I said in a soothing tone and placed my hand on his arm. "The invitations were already decided on before you even said anything to me. There's no way your comment would have caused them to change who they were going to pick."

"Couldn't it?" he shot back. "They're able to tell if you open the damn thing with just a prick of your finger!" He held up his own hand, showing me a small wound on his finger; the same as mine.

"Wait," I grabbed his hand and pulled it closer to inspect the wound. "You were invited too?"

Marsha shrugged. "I'm the eldest son of four, all my brothers are under ten, I was bound to be picked this time."

My brow furrowed at his words. "What do you mean? Why does it matter who you are?"

This time it was Marsha's turn to be confused. "Wait, I thought you knew about the Election. You acted like it yesterday."

I gave a guilty shrug. "I lied."

Marsha seemed surprised, as though he'd never been lied to before. Instead of letting him question me about my ethics, I decided to do a little questioning of my own.

"So," - I crossed my arms over my chest - "since now you know I don't know anything about this Election thing, why don't you fill in the blanks. No one else seems to want to."

"Did your stepmother not explain it to you? Before you opened the letter?" Marsha seemed even more amazed at their lack of cooperation than at my having lied to him. He must not get out much. Either that or people were really careful around him.

"No." I sighed in frustration. "It seems this Election thing is a big deal for them, or whatever." I glared down at the floor as I remembered how my stepfamily had behaved the night before. If they knew what was good for them, they'd stay away from me in the immediate future. What little future I had left until they came for me, anyway.

"Well, look," Marsha glanced down at the watch on his wrist, "we don't have much time until they come for us, but I'll do what I can to fill you in. But I'm afraid I don't know too much myself."

That was disheartening. If even the Soft Hands didn't know all the details and they wanted to go, then I wasn't sure what I could expect. Nothing good for sure.

"So, I've gathered only kids over seventeen get invited, right?" I asked, and Marsha nodded. "So, is it every family? Or only a select few? How exactly are they chosen?"

Marsha grimaced. "We don't really know. We do know they only invite those from families with more than one child. Maybe they want to make sure the lineage carries on?"

"Maybe." I mused. "What else? What should we expect at this party? We just dress up, hang out with the head honchos, and then we all go home?"

"No one knows."

"What do you mean no one knows?" I argued, getting irritated by the lack of information. "If it happens every year, surely someone has revealed what happened at the party when they came home, haven't they?"

Marsha's gaze went to the floor, his silence causing a sinking feeling in my stomach.

"Marsha," I urged. "Why doesn't anyone know?"

Finally, after what seemed like forever, Marsha answered. And it wasn't what I wanted to hear. "No one knows what happens because most don't come back," he explained, almost reluctant to tell me.

"And those who do?" I asked, my heart racing, almost positive he was about to tell me something horrific. Before he could tell me, another knock came at the door.

Both of our heads turned, but while my face held confusion, Marsha was afraid. "Clara, they're here."

Chapter 4

THIS TIME THE KNOCK on the door roused my stepfamily. They rushed down the stairs, their feet pounding on each step in their excitement.

When my two stepsisters landed at the bottom, where Marsha and I still stood, they only gave us a single passing glance before making a dash for the door. My stepmother seemed slightly less in a hurry though she did give me a disapproving glance as she followed her daughters.

"Do you think it's them?" Lea asked, her eyes wide and her hands wringing in front of her. She practically bounced on her heels making her pale blue knee-length dress flounce up and down like a hot air balloon.

"Who else would it be, you imbecile?" Julianna sneered, her hand going for the door.

"Julianna!" Belinda chastised, causing the older girl to pull her hand back with a snap. "We do not call people names in this house. We are not from the Glade."

"Sorry, mother." Julianna hung her head, not even bothered that her mother had practically insulted me in the same breath as she'd corrected her daughter.

"Now, we will answer the door like the civilized people we are." Belinda smoothed her hands down her own dress made of dark green material with tiny buttons all the way down the back. I wondered briefly if she had made it herself or if she had had one of her many workers do it for her. It was hard to imagine Belinda doing any kind of labor other than shouting orders, which she seemed to do so well.

Without having to ask, her daughters moved to the side allowing her to open the door which had endured further knocking during their skirmish. When it opened, it revealed a tall man, the tallest I'd ever seen, with dark-colored eyes and pale white hair, though he couldn't have been more than thirty. He gave a delighted grin which made his eyes twinkle in the sunlight.

"Pardon me for the intrusion, I am Malcolm," he said with a faint lilted accent.

"Oh, no trouble at all," my stepmother cooed and bowed slightly to the man, though I had no idea why. There was no indication that he was anyone of importance but maybe she knew more than she let on. "We were just wondering when you might be coming. Please let me welcome you to our home." She swept her arm into the doorway with an exaggerated flare. "Would you like some tea? Maybe something to eat?"

Malcolm smiled even more but shook his head. "No, no tea. I'm quite alright. I am simply here to pick up our guest." His eyes shifted over to where I stood and when they fell on Marsha, his expression brightened even more. "Ah, it looks like you have saved me a trip, Mr. Butchen. I was on my way to pick you up next."

My stepfamily's gaze landed on Marsha who ducked his head, his ears turning a bright red. "I was just checking on Clara since she just moved here."

"Oh, is that so?" Malcolm's eyes moved to land on me, scanning my form. If he saw anything of interest he didn't show it on his face, only that growingly creepy smile stayed in place. "Well, I imagine you will be quite a breath of fresh air compared to the others."

His comment made my stepsisters giggle. They sounded like birds squawking in their nests. At that moment, I was happy I would be leaving; at least then I would get a break from the two girls and their constant pestering.

"Are you ready to leave?" Malcolm turned his attention to Belinda as if she could answer for us. "Said all your goodbyes?"

"Actually," I started to speak up, hoping maybe I could convince him to allow me to see my father first but my stepmother cut me off with a glare.

"Yes! Everything is ready, and they can't wait to get going, right, Clarabelle?" The warning in her voice made me frown, my eyes narrowing into slits but what could I do? While I was in her house, she made the rules and no matter how much my father would disapprove there wasn't much I could do about it until he came back. I would just have to hope I could find someone at the Core who would take pity on a girl who was missing her father.

"Yes." I sighed in defeat and started toward the door. "We're ready. Right, Marsha?" I cocked a brow as I glanced back at the burly boy who hadn't stopped staring at Malcolm.

"Sure, sure," he muttered and came up to my side.

Malcolm clapped his hands together with glee and gestured out the door. "Then, by all means, let us be on our way. There are a few more to pick up on our way to the Core."

I followed him out of the door and down the small set of steps of my stepmother's home only to stop and gasp. A car stood before me and not just any car, a limousine.

Vehicles of any kind were rare in the Inner Circle, even more so in the Glade. The delivery truck my father and his assistant drove was the only vehicle I'd ever seen up close. Since I'd move to the Inner Circle, I'd seen a few but none as nice as the one before me.

Malcolm stopped at the door and opened it for us, gesturing inside. "Please, after you."

I glanced back at Marsha with a frown. Then, ignoring the nagging feeling in my stomach, I slid into the car.

The seats were made of shiny leather, and the inside smelled of fresh cut roses. It made my nose tickle, and I let out a loud sneeze. Rubbing my nose on the back of my sleeve, I moved further in so that Marsha could sit beside me.

"Wow." He gaped, a bit more stunned than I had been.

The door shut behind him and locked making my eyes jump to it. Malcolm didn't get into the back with us but sat in the passenger seat next to the driver. The window between the front and the back lowered revealing the two.

"Please, buckle your seat belts. We have two more to pick up on our way to the Core." His voice still held that I'm-so-happy-to-do-my-job type of tone, but now that we were in the car and away from prying eyes, it held a sort of warning edge to it. It seemed we had changed from guests to prisoners in a matter of seconds.

After I buckled my belt, which took some doing since I'd never been in a car before, my eyes scanned the rest of the car. The back section where Marsha and I sat, held two long seats facing each other, with a third set of seats placed against the wall where the window had risen back up. A small rectangular shaped box sat on the left side of the car, and before I could decide if I wanted to open it, Marsha beat me to it.

"Hey, it's a refrigerator." He laughed and took a bottle of water out of it.

Refrigerators weren't hard to come by. The whole of Alban had more electricity than anything else. In the Glade, we didn't use it more than to keep our food fresh and to see our meager plates in the evening light. The Soft Hands, on the other hand, had things like television and radios. They spent their evenings and weekends stuck in front of them just wasting the hours away.

I couldn't imagine doing such things. My stepsisters tried to convince me into watching one of their programs, but it only took me a whole of five minutes before I became restless. I was used to working with my hands, used to moving about; I couldn't stay in one place for hours at a time. It would drive me mad. I had a feeling the castle wouldn't be any better.

"I wouldn't get too comfortable," I muttered to Marsha who happily sipped away on his water, all thoughts of his previous warning gone.

"Why not?" he asked, not bothered that Malcolm and the driver could hear him. "We're their guests. They aren't going to do anything to us on the way there."

The way he said it made me start. "What do you mean?"

Marsha's face closed, and he capped his bottle. "Never mind, I don't want to worry you. I'm sure it will be fine." He smiled slightly and took my hand in his. It was warm and a bit clammy from the bottle, but I didn't pull away right away. Not until we stopped again with a jerk.

The window separating up lowered again, and Malcolm turned his smiling face to us. "We are stopping briefly to get another one of our guests, and then we have one more, and we'll be well on our way to the Core. Sit tight, and I'll be right back."

The window rolled back up before either of us could say anything. We sat in the back of the limo, neither of us daring to speak. I didn't know why Marsha had clammed up, but I didn't have much to say, at least not to Marsha who was in the same situation as I was. He had as much power as I did. Which to be honest wasn't much.

After a few minutes, the door to the limo unlocked and in stepped a petite blonde-haired beauty. Her hair curled down over her shoulder and lay on the top of her rose-colored dress. The small smile on her lips never wavered as she buckled in across from us.

"Hey, Tillie," Marsha greeted.

The girl glanced over at him and nodded, "Hello. It's a nice day, isn't it?"

"Yes, it is," Marsha replied as if it were all normal. I watched on in confusion as Tillie stared out the window dreamily as if we weren't even there.

When the car started again, I leaned over to Marsha and whispered, "What's wrong with her?"

"That's the part I was trying to tell you about before," he answered, this time having the smarts to keep his voice down. "If you don't get selected to stay, they send you back but without any memory of what happened."

"So, you will end up like that?" I eyed Tillie who had started to watch her hands move through the air.

"No." Marsha shook his head. "That's because Tillie is the oldest child. Her brother is only two, so she's been picked every year for the last four years."

"And she's been sent back every time?" I asked with disbelief.

"Yes, which is why she's ... not quite all there," he ended politely.

I sat back in my seat at his explanation, none of it making sense. If they didn't want Tillie the first four times, then why would they keep inviting her?

"It's because of my looks," Tillie answered my unspoken question, surprising me. "Oh, don't look so scared," she giggled. "I'm not psychic, but everyone always asks every year."

"Wait," I put my hand out and moved to the edge of my seat, "I thought you don't remember what happens there?"

"Oh, I don't," she smiled. "But I do remember being picked up with the others and every time they ask the same question." She sighed as if it were a burden to explain. "I'm pretty, you see, much prettier than I should be and that's why they keep inviting me. But not after this year." She giggled again as if she had a secret to tell.

"Why not?" I glanced at her and Marsha. "Why not after this year?"

"Because I'll be twenty-one and I will be too old to be invited." She replied with a happy sound before her eyes were distracted by something outside. "Oh, look! We're here."

Marsha and I froze in our seat as the limo came to a stop, but we weren't in front of the palace. We were picking up another guest. This girl wasn't as remarkable as Tillie and complained as she entered the back.

"I have to share a car with them?" she cried out as she flopped down on the seat. "Some honored guest." She muttered under her breath as she adjusted her gown. She kept her dark hair short on the sides with a long bit on top falling over her viper green eyes. Shiny earrings filled her ears while her nose bore a single piercing. The gown she wore would have been called sexy on a less busty person, but on her, it became almost obscene.

"What are you staring at?" The girl snapped at me, studying my own outfit. "Is that what you are going to wear?" The sheer outrage in her voice made me realize Marsha and I were the only ones not dressed up, but even he looked better than I did in yesterday's rumpled clothes. He'd discarded his apron before we'd entered the limo and now sat in his white shirt and slacks.

I shrugged a shoulder. "They invited *me*, not the other way around."

The girl scoffed and ran a hand through her hair. "Well, that's fine by me. You keep thinking that way. Makes my job easier."

I frowned at her words and almost asked what she meant, but she beat me to it.

"I'm Zara, by the way. Remember it because I'm the one who's going to win this thing."

Chapter 5

"WIN THIS THING?" I asked, shooting a look at Marsha who only shrugged. "Win what?"

Zara fluffed her skirts with an impatient huff. "You know, the big prize. The position above all other positions." When I still only stared at her, she let out a haughty laugh. "You really don't know anything, do you?"

I shook my head and shrugged again. I seemed to be doing that a lot lately. I didn't like it.

"This," Zara circled her finger around the limo, "is all a ruse to pick new people to live in their palace. To live there as servants, or as more pleasurable company." The last part she said with a sultry tone and winked in Marsha's direction. He shifted next to me and blushed.

"How do you know all this?" I asked leaning slightly forward in my seat. "I thought no one knew about the party."

Zara lifted a shoulder as she eyeballed her nails. "I'm not just anyone. My father is the mayor of this little hovel, and I'm privy to all sorts of information. Like, how I know you, Clarabelle," she sneered, too happy with herself about knowing my name, "aren't from here."

"So?" I cocked a brow at her.

"So," she drew out, "you shouldn't have been invited. There must have been some kind of mistake. It was Julianna's turn. I know it. I saw the list."

"The list?" Marsha and I asked at the same time and then exchanged a confused look.

Zara leaned back in her seat, her hands clasped in her front her gleefully. "Oh, you didn't know about the list?" She didn't wait for us to answer before she continued. "You thought the invitation was sent out at random, do you? Not so." She waved a finger in front of her. "My father sends a list of eligible candidates to the Core, and they send out the invitation from that list. And your name," - she pointed a finger at me - "wasn't on it. I saw it."

My lips curled down in confusion. If my name wasn't on the list, then how did I get an invitation? If I shouldn't here, then why was I? Someone must have added my name, but the question was who? And why?

"But it doesn't matter anyway," Zara cooed as the limo came to a stop once more.

"And why is that?" I asked but was interrupted by the window in the front as it began to descend.

Malcolm's smiling face appeared, his large white teeth gleaming. "We're here!"

Everyone turned to peer out the darkened windows, our eyes straining to see beyond the small frame. There wasn't much there to see; tall pillars rose up supporting the roof of the majestic covered entrance. People, likely servants in their pristine matching dark gray outfits, stood in two straight lines stopping just a few feet from the limo. When the door opened on Marsha's side, I peered over his shoulders at a blood-red carpet running between the two lines of people.

Marsha unsnapped his seat belt quick as can be and hopped out of the car door. I struggled with mine for a moment before I finally got it off. Tillie exited before me, but as I tried to leave Zara pulled me back, her nails biting into my arm.

"Remember, you aren't supposed to be here, so don't get any ideas. I'm still going to be winning this thing," she snarled at me, her eyes flashing.

I jerked my arm away from her with a condescending smile. "Then you have nothing to worry about." Her face lit up in surprise, but I didn't wait to hear what else she had to say.

I stepped out of the car, and my booted foot sank into the plush red carpet as my eyes widened. This close to the castle, the building was a lot bigger than it seemed. The place had to be fifty or sixty feet high, and there were so many windows I wondered if I would be able to see my house in the Glade from one of them.

As I gaped at the palace, Zara shoved into my side, pushing me into one of the servants. The woman I fell into could have been my mother, with her dark hair streaked white and equally dark eyes. The small smile on her face as she helped me back to my feet caught me off guard. There was something about her, something which made me want to trust her with all my darkest secrets.

"Thank you, Venna," Malcolm came up from behind and placed a hand on my shoulder making my back stiffen. His arrival caused Venna's smile to fall and her eyes to hit the floor. I wanted to stay and talk to her, to find out what all this was, but Malcolm was steering me away from her and the procession of servants.

He led me into the palace at a quick pace, not allowing me to linger to take in the wonder around me. I tried my best to keep up with him, his long legs giving him the advantage over my five-foot-six frame. When we finally stopped before a door, I realized none of the other people I had arrived with were in sight.

"Where'd everyone else go?" I asked peering into the room before me.

"Do not worry, you will see them later." Malcolm smiled that over-exaggerated smile of his and then for a moment his face darkened. "Now, I'm only going to tell you once. Do not mingle with the help. They have a job to do, and they can't help you."

"Help me?" I frowned. "If it hadn't been for Venna, I would have fallen flat on my face. I think they helped me plenty already."

Malcolm made a sound which could have been a laugh, but I couldn't be sure. "Oh, you are going to be a fun one, I can already tell." Then his sparkling smile came back into place, and he gave me a little shove. "Now, go get ready and remember what I said, or you'll be sorry."

I turned to glare at him for pushing me, but he was already gone. My eyes searched down the hallway we had come down but couldn't find any clue as to where he could have gone. Shrugging, I spun back around to the room waiting for me.

Twice the size of the room I had back at my stepmother's home, it could hold my entire house in the Glade inside it. The bed was far bigger than I could ever need, and the wardrobe probably held clothes I would never imagine wearing. I walked across the room and picked up a strange cylinder-shaped brush. Just as I wondered what it was for a chorus of squeals erupted from behind me.

Spinning around, my eyes grew larger at the three women coming toward me. Dressed in black from head to toe, from sexy barely-there slip-of-a-dresses to prim-and-proper suits, they each had their own style. They crowded around me all talking at once as they rattled off the different attributes of my appearance they adored. From my long untouched hair to my perfectly sized breasts, there was nothing about me too private to discuss.

My head was spinning as they turned me this way and that, until a series of snaps filled the air. The women withdrew from me and, like moths to a flame, floated across the room to where a man stood.

Also, cased in black, his pale skin stood out against the collar of his shirt. His eyes were a strange orange shade, which seemed to call me to them. Lips quirked up into a smirk, he reached for the women as they seemed to drape themselves over him.

"You must be Clarabelle." His voice, like soft silk against my skin, touched my ears. The women sighed in unison as if hearing him speak were a gift of itself.

I'd never been one for pretty men, or ones who had such a pull on those around them. I didn't have time for them … or rather, most of them didn't have time for me. Back in the Glade, most of us were too worried about surviving to think about finding love. Of course, eventually, we found it one way or another, or we'd have died out. Nevertheless, now was not the time to be thinking of pretty men; not with what's at stake.

"Yes." I nodded but then added for good measure, "but it's Clara, actually."

His eyes widened slightly, but his smirk never wavered as he shook his adorers off and strode toward me. "So, Clara," - he started circling me like a vulture - "you are a lot prettier than I thought you would be."

"Uh, thanks," I answered, not sure where his thoughts were going. Compared to my stepsisters, I wasn't that much more than plain, but I supposed I did have a sort of prettiness to me. My father often said I looked like my mother when she had been my age. I'd always thought my mother was beautiful, but I'd never thought of myself in that way.

"But I do have to say, I am disappointed in your choice in wardrobe." He plucked at the sleeves of my shirt, making the women giggle.

"I wasn't told there was a dress code." I shrugged as watched him out of the corner of my eye.

"Oh, there's not," he reassured me. "But most of the guests tend to arrive in more ..." He waved his hand in the air around my outfit and then sighed. "... just more."

"Sorry to disappoint you," I growled, tired of being surveyed like a cow for breeding. "I'm sorry, but you haven't told me who you are? Any of you." I glanced around him to the trio waiting by the door.

The man seemed positively embarrassed at my question. Something I doubt he felt often.

"I apologize for not introducing myself sooner." He bowed slightly with a long flourish of his arms. "My name is Asher, and I will be your guide, so to speak, for the duration of your stay."

"Guide?" My brows furrowed. "What do I need a guide for? It's just a party." Except it wasn't just a party. Zara had told me as much, but I still couldn't get it out of my head that I'd just go to this thing and be home by the time my father returned. A foolish notion for sure.

"Oh no," one of the women, the one in the slinky dress, came forward with a shake of her head, "It's not just a party. First, there's the first impression, then—"

"Then there's the interview." Another one of the women, who wore a daring pantsuit with a low neckline, stepped in.

"And then finally, the party itself where you will be selected for your position," the last women with a high collared dress added.

"And I will be there to help you every step of the way," Asher finished with a wink.

"As well as your" - I gestured my head toward the women - "groupies?"

That had been the wrong thing to say. The three women's face contorted in anger and they started toward me before Asher held a hand up, stopping them in their tracks.

"Now, you are new here, so I will give you the benefit of the doubt, but these women are not groupies. They are my companions and closest confidants, and I won't have you offending them again, are we clear?" Asher scolded, a bit of a bite to his tone.

"Of course." I nodded and then looked at the women. "I'm sorry. I didn't mean anything by it."

They seemed to simmer down at my apology and then Asher came up to me, taking me by the shoulders. "Now that that's out of the way, let's get you ready to be presented."

The way he said it, with a gleam in his eye, made me wish I was back home, cleaning the stables. Anywhere but here with this madman and his wild ideas of fashion.

Chapter 6

PLUCKED, SCRUBBED, AND WAXED in every possible way - Asher never thought I was clean enough - I got over my embarrassment over my nudity in front of the man after he showed no more than a clinical interest in my body. In any case, his companions, as he'd called them, spent more time touching me than he ever did.

While they followed Asher's every instruction to get me ready, I managed to learn that the giggling women had names. The woman with the opinion of the-more-skin-revealed-the-better called herself Neeka. Streaks of blue colored her blonde hair, and she wore a dark shade of lipstick which didn't wash out her skin the way I would have thought it might.

The one who favored suits liked to wear her hair slicked back so that she almost looked more masculine than female. Willow, she told me, was her name. She didn't talk as much as the other two, but what she did say was insightful, making me instantly like her.

The last of the women, Rosel, named for her naturally red lips, favored more of a prudish look. It caused her and the others to argue as they tried to figure out what I should wear. Eventually, though, Asher stepped in.

"I think this one would do nicely," he said as he withdrew a long black dress which sparkled in the light.

"It's beautiful," I commented, fingering the sequined material. I only even knew what it was made of from being in my stepmother's shop. Back in the Glade, cotton was about all we had to work with.

"Good." Asher handed the gown to Rosel who held it open for me to step into. Asher took my hand and helped me slid the gown up and over my bare skin. It fit like a glove, and as they zipped me into it, I found it harder to breathe.

"It is supposed to be so tight?" I asked, taking small breaths.

"Beauty is pain," he snickered and led me carefully over to the mirror. "See what a little bit of care will do for such a rare flower as you?"

I stepped in front of the three-way mirror and was stunned. They had painted my face with makeup, something I had never used in my life, and now my eyes looked large and sultry. My lips were liquid red, but when I pressed my fingers to my mouth, it didn't rub away. The dress itself hugged my body in all the right places, pushing my chest up and giving the illusion that I had more hips than I really did. Overall, I didn't look like myself at all. I looked like one of them.

"It's great," I answered, not wanting to hurt their feelings. What I really wanted to say was that I hated it. I wanted to put my own clothes back on and wash my face off, become the girl I had been before I had stepped through those doors. But I couldn't. They expected me to play their little game, which included a uniform. This was all it was, another part of the game.

The trio nodded in agreement as they patted themselves on the back for their work. Asher watched my face as if he didn't quite believe me, but after a moment, he let it go and ushered me toward the bedroom door.

"Now, this first part is really simple. You follow the person in front of you and then leave when told. This is just so they can get a look at you, nothing more." His words were meant to be reassuring, I was sure, but they only made me more confused. I still didn't know exactly what I was doing here. What I was being paraded around for.

"Have you thought about what position you want?" Asher asked as he walked me down the hall while his companions remained behind in the room. I was thankful for that; I couldn't handle any more of their giggling or dreamy eyes. They might be Asher's companions, but they sure seemed more like girlfriends than anything to me.

When I realized Asher was still waiting for me to answer, I chewed on my cheek until I winced. "I don't know, really. What are they again?" I hoped he couldn't tell how lost I was. Zara seemed to know all the answers, but Marsha had been like me, not knowing much of anything.

Or maybe that was what he wanted you to think. He could be playing it close to the chest because he saw me as competition and didn't want me to beat him. The thought swirled in my head, making me doubt even myself.

"There are only three positions you can be chosen for. If you don't get picked for any of them, you'll be sent home," Asher explained.

"Like Tillie."

Asher frowned at her name and then nodded. "Yes, like Tillie. That poor girl. They should have just left her alone after the first two times, but those bastards can be sadistic when they want to be."

The way he talked about them made me mad. If their own people thought they were messed up, then what hope did I have? There had to be some way to appeal to their humanity. Some way to help the Glade and to get back home in one piece.

"Tillie said it's 'cause she's pretty," I said, suddenly needing to know as much as possible about what was happening. "Is that what it takes? Is that all they care about? What this is all about?" I held my arms out to the side, twirling slightly making the skirt at my ankles swirl.

Stopping in the middle of the hallway, Asher took me by the elbow, making me stumble over the three-inch heels they had made me wear. "Listen, Clarabelle—"

"Clara."

Asher pressed his lips together and gave me a look. "Look, the girls and I think you are a blast. A regular breath of fresh air compared to a lot of the guests who come through here, but you're going to have a hard time if you don't stop asking so many questions."

I clenched my jaw in frustration. "But if I don't ask questions, how am I supposed to know what's going on? You guys don't exactly give a manual for Election etiquette."

My sponsor sighed and then glanced up and down the hallway. There weren't many people. Most of them were servants in the dark gray outfits, and they didn't give us much of a passing glance. When he seemed to think it was safe, he lowered his voice as he said, "I'm going to do you a favor. Something I never do for any other guest."

"Alright?" I lifted a now-perfectly sculpted brow.

"There are three positions available to you. You can be a servant," - he pointed to a passing gray-clad man - "a companion like my girls, or ..."

"Or?"

"A convert." His voice went very low on the last one, and his eyes became serious.

"What's a convert? Like to a religion?" I shook my head trying to take in everything he was telling me.

"No, not a religion." He waved his hands between us. "A convert will be someone who will be inducted into the Fold."

"What?" I gasped loudly, causing a few people to glance our way. I quickly lowered my voice, ducking my head down. "I didn't know that was possible. Aren't they, like, all-powerful?"

Asher snorted. "They wish. And no, it's not usual. It only happens once every few decades when those in the Fold wish for a ..." - he seemed to mull over his word choice before finally settling on - "lover or spouse, you could say. That's the only way anyone ever gets in."

I groaned. "Why does everything have to do with marrying up? First my father and now this? Can't I just get my memory wiped now and go home?"

Shaking his head, he grasped me by the shoulders with a smile. "Sorry Clara doll, but someone found you interesting enough to invite. I think it will be a bit hard to get sent home now."

"So," I sighed, crossing my arms over my chest, "what if I don't want to be any of those things. Can I just make sure I don't attract any of their attention? Would that make sure I go home?"

"You could try," Asher mused. "But" - he brushed my hair away from my face - "with a face like that, the likelihood of going home free and clear is a fantasy."

"Why? Tillie did. Four times, I might add."

"That was different," Asher said but didn't elaborate. He took me by the arm, and we headed down the hallway once more. "All I can tell you is decide for yourself what kind of person you want to be here. Do you want to serve, befriend, or rule? Either way, you are here to stay, I would bet my life on it."

I chewed on the inside of my cheek as we came upon a group of equally spiffed-up guests. I caught sight of Tillie and Marsha who smiled and came my way. Thankfully, Zara was nowhere in sight. I didn't think I could deal with her attitude right now.

"Hey, Clara. You look great." Marsha's eyes roamed over my form, a blush filling his face. I didn't know how I had thought he could lie to me; he couldn't keep his emotions to himself if he wanted to.

I smiled and nodded toward his tailored suit. "Thanks, you do too."

He chuckled. "Yeah, who knew there was a dashing gentleman underneath all that cow blood and sweat?"

Asher made a face and shuddered slightly.

"Marsha's a butcher," I explained with a small smile. "He handles all the meat for the Inner Circle."

"And the Core," Marsha added, looking proud of himself.

"That's great," Asher commented, though his voice said how unimpressed he was. His eyes turned from Marsha to land on Tillie. Taking her hand in his, Tillie's eyes met his, and a small smile graced her face. "Tillie, so good to see you again. I hope you are doing well?"

"I wish I could say the same. I'm sure we have met many times before, but sadly, I can't recall. But as far as how I'm doing," - her attention drifted away from us toward the double doors we were all waiting in front of - "I can hardly decide. They will open the doors soon, we should probably get ready."

Not at all bothered by her strangeness, Asher nodded sternly. "Too true. You should all prepare yourselves. This is the most important part, and as Tillie can attest," - he shot her a dashing smile - "looks are everything."

Just then, a lady with a large head of curls decorated with roses, called out, "Ladies and gentlemen, the Crimson Fold will now see you. Please form a single file line."

Tillie and Marsha moved away to get in line, but before I could join them, Asher grabbed my arm. Stopping in place, I turned back to my sponsor with a questioning look.

"I'm going to give you a bit of advice, and if I were you, I'd take it." His eyes scanned the growing line with a sort of anxiety on his face. "There are four times as many guests this year, meaning thirty-five other guests you have to compete against for a spot. Now, if I were you, I'd be aiming for the convert position and not just any position, *the* convert position."

"I don't understand." I glanced at the growing line and then back to him. The large-haired lady hustled everyone into place, and I was sure she'd be looking my way soon.

"There are two convert positions this year, and one of those positions is for none other than Patrick Blordril." I gasped, and he hushed me, but it was too late. Our hostess had heard me and started my way. "You want that position." Asher's grip dug into my arm, his eyes holding an intensity I'd only seen when he had been doing my nails. "No, Clarabelle Feldman, you need that position."

"But what if I don't want it?" I asked quickly, aware our time was running out.

"Oh, you are going to want it." Asher smiled knowingly. "And so, will plenty of the others."

"Come, come now." The big-haired lady stopped in front of us and tried to usher me away. "Asher, shame on you holding up the line." She wagged her finger playfully.

Asher placed a hand on his chest, half bowing with a look of contrition. "Daphne, you know I can't help myself."

Daphne waved him off with a flirtatious smile but kept pulling me the other direction. I glanced back over my shoulder toward Asher, and he mouthed two words.

Be careful.

Chapter 7

SINCE I HAD SPENT most of my time talking with Asher, I ended up near the end of the line, shoved between a small girl who barely looked twelve let alone seventeen and a long-legged red-hair boy. I didn't have time to make their acquaintance before Daphne threw open the doors.

My heart beat in my ears as each person went into the room. I was far enough down the line that I couldn't see much more than a bit of the deep burgundy wallpaper. But I could see the guests come out another set of doors further down the hallway. As they came out, someone directed them to another set of doors on the opposite side. Maybe a waiting room?

Zara was one of the first people to go through the line and come out the other side. A look of triumph lit her makeup-covered face, and she flounced into the other room without prompting. A short while later, Tillie came floating out, her usual dreamy expression still firmly in place.

When Marsha came through, he wasn't smiling. He didn't seem happy at all. In fact, from where I stood he seemed upset, maybe even angry. I'd never seen the butcher boy in such a state. He'd always had a smile for everyone he met, even my stepmother. It made me wonder what in the room could have upset him so.

I didn't have to wait too much longer to have my chance to find out. Soon there were only two people in front of me, and I could finally see into the room.

From where I stood, the room had to be three times the size of the bedroom they had given me and even more extravagantly decorated. The heavy drapes were drawn, but there was enough lighting from the crystal chandelier that the outside light wouldn't be needed. Though I imagined by now it would be early evening, there wouldn't be much light coming through.

"Come on, dear," Daphne placed a hand on my shoulder and tottered up to the door.

I tried to control my breathing as I took in the sight before me. A long table lined the opposite wall, twelve people filling the seats behind it. Each of them had a face of stone and a glass in front of them. Every once in a while, one would drink from the glass, but for the most part, they were still. My eyes searched down the line, taking in the young faces of those who made of the Crimson Fold. When they landed on Patrick Blordril, my breath caught.

I'd only ever seen him on fliers, but he was even more otherworldly in person. He wore his hair slicked back, the color so white it could have only been from age, except he didn't look much older than thirty. His eyes were just as pale, and I almost thought he might be blind, but the way his eyes followed the tall fellow in front of me told me they worked very well.

When the tall boy left the room, all their eyes turned to me. It was my turn now.

"Just walk to the x taped on the floor." Daphne pointed out a black spot on the floor a few feet away from the table. "Do a slow spin and then exit the other door. Got it?" She locked eyes with me, and I nodded though I couldn't breathe.

As I wobbled from the doorway, my eyes kept straying back to Patrick's, making me even more unbalanced. Before I even made it halfway to the designated spot, my ankle turned sideways, and I almost fell over. Nerves shot and thoroughly fed up, I stopped in my tracks.

Hiking my skirt up, I chucked off my heels and stomped over to the tapped spot. I turned to the watching members, spun around quickly, and then gave a mock bow. As I came back up, my eyes locked with Patrick's again, and this time, there was a hint of a smile on his lips.

Caught off guard by his smile, I stayed a moment too long on the x, making Daphne hiss at me. Glancing her way, I realized my mistake and promptly marched toward the other door. When I got there, my feet hitting the soft cushion, I stopped.

"My shoes!" I cried out and tried to go back, but the person on my side of the door caught me and forced me to go in the other direction.

Sighing unhappily, I entered the room where the other guests were waiting. Almost an exact mirror of the other room, but instead of a waiting line of judges at the table, there was a wide display of food. All the other guests who had gone before me were in varies states of eating or sitting around in lush chairs. Some of them were chatting amongst themselves while others watched with hawk-like gazes as if any of us could strike at any moment.

"Clara!" Marsha's voice called out to me, and I walked over to where he sat with Tillie and two other guests.

"Hi." I waved slightly at him and Tillie.

"This is Narq and Violet." Marsha gestured toward the tall boy who had been in front of me in line, and a small girl with eyes the color of amethysts. She had to be Violet, or the boy had some strange parents.

I nodded to them and then sat on the edge of the couch next to Tillie. A servant came up to me and offered me a glass of something bubbling and yellow. Taking the drink, I took a big gulp. The liquid tingled on the way down making me cough.

The others laughed while Tillie patted me on the back.

Thanking her, I gasped, "What is that?"

"Champagne," Narq told me with a laugh. "Haven't you ever had it before?"

I shook my head my eyes watering. "No, we don't have alcohol where I live."

"Where you live?" Violet asked her eyes lighting up with interest. "How could you not have alcohol? It's everywhere in the Inner Circle. I'm lucky to keep it out of the house and away from my mother." A kind of sadness filled the small girl's eyes, and she reminded me of a girl I used to work with back home.

Lira.

While I didn't have any siblings, I'd kind of adopted her as my little sister. I taught her how to plant the seed and even let her help deliver a calf. She was the closest thing to a sister and a friend I'd ever had. Lira had been a sad creature too. She'd rarely smiled, and when she did, there was still an underlying frailty to her.

Later, when I found out she had an ailing little sister at home, I did everything in my power to make sure she had fun. Even if I could only get a little smile or giggle out of her, I felt it made up for the misery she had to go back home to. Then one day, when she didn't come to work, I went to her home only to find out her sister, who had only been four, had passed away. The family was taking a day off to mourn and bury her. I went home myself and cried like I hadn't since my own mother had passed away.

The next day Lira was back in the fields working, but she didn't talk for weeks. No matter how much I tried to make her smile or laugh, she wouldn't. Then I stopped trying and just did my work. Eventually, she got better, but I could still see the effects of her sister's death on her. I understood better than most, but even I had a hard time comforting her. I just did my best to make her day brighter, which was all any of us could do for each other.

I wondered if Violet had someone in her life who helped her day get brighter.

"Clara is from the Glade," Marsha answered for me. I shot him a look, but he ignored me. I hadn't wanted to tell anyone. It would make me stand out more amongst the other guests, which would only make me an even bigger threat to those who wanted to win the convert position. No matter what Asher thought, I just wanted to stay under the radar, hope they got bored with me and sent me home.

"Where are your shoes? Did someone take them?" Tillie asked, only slightly focused on my bare feet.

"Uh, no." I rubbed one foot over the other, my face heating. "I kind of kicked them off in there."

"What?" Violet giggled, coughing in her drink. "You took off your shoes in front of them?"

I winced and took another drink of my champagne, the burn settled into my stomach making me feel pleasantly light. "Yeah, well, they made me trip."

Tillie's reminder about my shoes made me realize how utterly useless it was to hope I would go unnoticed. Fat chance of that now. My little show at the first impressions would definitely make me stand out.

"I would have loved to have seen their faces!" Narq laughed and smacked Marsha on the arm. "Those snooty Fold members probably wet themselves laughing. Can you imagine?"

God, I hope not. Though I hadn't paid much attention to the table of judges, the gaze of Patrick following my every move came to mind. Had he laughed at my little act of defiance after I left the room? Did he even care?

I shook my head and stared into my drink. What was wrong with me? I'd decided I wasn't going to be anyone's anything and here I was daydreaming about the leader of this whole freak show.

"Well, I'm not surprised in the least," Zara sneered as she sauntered up to us. Her outfit clung to her body like a second skin, the shiny black material of her body suit made a faint squeaking noise as she moved. The ensemble was topped off with knee-high boots which could be a weapon themselves considering how many spikes covered them.

"What do you want, Zara?" I asked, slightly distracted as I tried to figure out how she even got into that thing.

Zara responded with a nasty grin and laced her fingers in front of her. "I just wanted to come over and see how it went, but I can see I was right in thinking you aren't supposed to be here. Only someone from the Glade would lose their shoes in the middle of such an important moment." She sniffed, her gaze going up and down my form with distaste. "I'm sure they are writing your name down now to send you packing."

"Fine with me," I countered. "I wouldn't want to rain on your parade, though," I grinned, scanning over her plastic clothes. "You seemed to have that covered."

The others laughed at my joke, but Zara didn't seem to think it was funny. Stepping forward, she pointed a finger at my chest. "You think you are so clever, but when I'm sitting at the right hand of the most powerful man in all of Alban, I'll send you and your father packing back to the Glade. Or better yet, the Wilds."

Her threat didn't bother me. I'd be happy to go back to the Glade, though, but the Wilds was another story. No one really knew what lay beyond the edge of the Glades. There were wild animals which could be hunted if one were brave enough. Most people stayed away from the edge; they would rather starve in the Glade than die in the wilderness.

Hardly a choice to me.

I opened my mouth to tell her where she could stick her threat but was interrupted when Daphne entered the room and called us to her.

"Come, come now, it's time to see how you did." Her voice held a chipper tone to it as she pointed a remote at the wall. A black screen lowered from the paneling near the ceiling before it lit up and a scoreboard with the title *Election Day One Results.*

"Finally," Zara growled shoving away from me and heading toward the screen with the rest of the other guests. I didn't have much interest in seeing how I had done, not unless it was going to help me go home. So, when Marsha stopped in front of me, his hand held out, I frowned.

Not waiting for me to take it, he pulled me up from my seat and said, "Come on, let's watch Zara's face as you wipe her off the board."

Chapter 8

ALL THIRTY-SIX GUESTS WERE listed on the board, in no particular order it seemed. Beside each name was a different colored number. There wasn't a legend to tell what any of it meant, but somehow everyone else seemed to know.

As each person found their name, they either cheered or groaned in response. I searched out my name on the list and found it between two others I didn't recognize. Next to it sat the number nine in dark red.

Just as I had thought. I'd done horribly. My little stunt with the shoes had caused my horrible score, and now they would have to send me home. For some reason, I wasn't as relieved to go home as I'd thought

I would be. Patrick's penetrating eyes came back to mind, but I shook them off. Obviously, I hadn't made as much of an impression on him as he had made on me.

Just for curiosity's sake, I looked for Marsha and Tillie's names. Marsha scored a seven, but his number was purple, while Tillie had earned a four in pale pink. I glanced up to Marsha who still stood by my side and saw the confusion on his face as well.

"Well," I patted his arm. "I guess I don't really want to see the look on Zara's face." I pointed at the board to where her name sat next to a bright orange five. "Though Tillie did better than her, so I guess that's something."

Marsha looked down at me frowning, "No, she didn't."

"What do you mean? Tillie got a five and Zara got a four. And my nine is red, so obviously that's bad. Right?" I gestured toward the screen, earning strange looks from those around me. Some of them were angry while others stared in wonder. What the heck was wrong with them?

Just then Violet came up beside me and grabbed my arm with a squeal. "Oh my god, did you see my score? I got a seven! I can't believe it." She shook me in her excitement but didn't seem to notice my confusion. "And did you see what color I got? Pink! It's not as good as Marsha's, but I'll take attractive over annoying yellow any day. What did you get?"

I stared down at her expectant eyes and then exchanged a look with Marsha who just shrugged. "Uh," I started. "I got a red nine."

The piercing squeal from Violet made my ears ring which only became worse when it was followed by an outraged cry. The crowd suddenly broke apart as a feral Zara shoved her way through, her eyes zeroing in on me.

I forced myself to stay put as she stomped across the room. "You," she snarled, her teeth bared. "What did you do to get a nine? Flash them?"

The reactions of those around me were starting to make me think I had everything wrong. Maybe my score wasn't on the low side? My eyes shot to the board once more, and I realized mine was the only nine and furthermore the highest number on the board.

Turning my attention back to Zara, I shrugged. "I guess they liked my Glade ways after all."

Zara's hands came up, her long nails sharpened into points but before she could wrap them around my neck, Daphne stepped in. "Now, ladies. Let's show some decorum, shall we?" She shot a warning look at Zara who glared before leaving in a huff.

With Zara gone, Daphne turned her attention to me. "Congratulations on your score, Clarabelle. You should be very proud." She touched a hand to my chin with a small smile before she spun around and addressed the rest of the room. "You can find a full report on the scoring back in your rooms. When you are ready, your sponsors will escort you back to discuss what you should do from there."

When Daphne left, I asked Marsha and Violet, "So a nine's good right?"

"Of course!" Violet smiled brightly. "You can only get as high as a ten, and you got a nine. That's the highest anyone has gotten in a long time."

I frowned at her explanation. "I thought no one knew much about the Election?"

"Well, no. Not really." Violet bit her lip and then looked up to Marsha. "Most of the stuff we know is just rumors, but sometimes someone's memory wipe doesn't stick, and then we can find out some things. Like the ranking system." She pointed toward the screen. "But usually they get taken away pretty quick and rewiped. Or worse." Her voice lowered at the last bit.

"Or worse?" I raised a brow.

This time Marsha answered, his arms crossed over his chest. "They don't come back. And if I were you, I'd be worried about yourself. Zara has it in for you, and if I know anything about her, she's a nasty piece of work and won't hesitate to find some way to sabotage you."

We all turned to where Zara ranted at two other girls. They seemed about as interested as a potato, but the fear in their eyes kept them from leaving the girl to complain on her own. Seemed like the judges weren't the only ones who found her annoying.

"Well," I sighed and raised a shoulder before dropping it, "If she wants to sabotage me, there isn't much I can do to stop her.

Though I'd gladly give her my score if it meant I could go home."

"Shh." Violet shushed me, her eyes darting around. "Don't let them hear you talk like that. The others are already a bit wary of you. You don't want to give them another reason to be against you."

I shifted my weight, my feet a little sore from the hard tile. "Why would they be wary of me?"

"'Cause you're from the Glade," Tillie answered coming up beside me. "Zara has been telling anyone who will listen about how your father bribed your way onto the list and now ..."

"With my high score, they think I paid for that too," I finished for her and groaned. "I don't think I can handle this anymore. I'm going to find Asher and go back to my room."

As I moved away from them, Marsha followed, catching me by the arm. "Hey, wait up."

"What now?" I wearily asked.

Marsha held his hands up in defense though I hadn't offered violence. I was too tired for that. But then again, I have been told that I get mean when I'm tired.

"I just wanted to warn you."

"About what?" I winced, even I knew that came out snippy. "I'm sorry, it's been a long day."

He nodded. "I know. So much has happened. It's funny to think we just got here this morning."

"Right." I agreed and then tried to make myself sound nicer. "So, what was it you wanted to tell me?"

Rubbing a hand on the back of his neck, his face brightened to that red shade he was so fond of. "Just that you should be careful. If you can, make some friends. Don't let Zara turn everyone against you, or you will be going home but not the way you want to." He gave me a knowing look before leaving me to return to the group.

I thought over what he said on my way to the door. I'd never been much good at making friends. Besides Lira, I pretty much kept to myself. Making people like me hadn't been something I got to practice at. I did my work, and people generally responded well in kind. Sure, that didn't mean I got invited to parties or the like, but we got along well. Well, enough that I wouldn't wish harm on any of them and I'd like to think they felt the same way.

Zara, on the other hand, could be a problem. I had a feeling her rumors were just the beginning, and if she could, she would find a way to really hurt me. Her almost-attack on me showed that.

When I left the room, Asher stood waiting. Relief swept over me when I realized he hadn't brought his little triage with him. I couldn't deal with their incessant giggling and talk of frivolous things.

"I would say that congratulations are in order." Asher smiled as he took my arm, then his eyes went to my bare feet. "What happened to your shoes?"

"It's a long story." I didn't elaborate as we walked through the hall. He chattered about some of the other guests' outfits and how he knew mine had made a difference in my score, but I wasn't really listening. Everything happened so fast, it was hard to imagine that just yesterday I had been sitting in the field eating an apple as I sneered at the fake grass. Now, I'd be lucky to ever see the outside again.

"Asher," I said, making him stop mid-sentence. "What made you come here?"

"What do you mean?" His brow furrowed, but it didn't make his face any less attractive. I wondered if he ever had a problem with that. Being attractive. I know I'd get tired of it.

"I mean, why are you here?" I gestured around the long ornate hallway. "Do you actually like all this?"

Asher laughed. "It's not as simple as like or not."

"Then what is it?"

"We all play a game, Clara. One that goes back to the beginning of time. We pretend to be someone different to fit in, to survive. What we do to stay alive isn't always something we like, but we do it anyway."

"So, you're just pretending to be my friend?" I peeked at him from the corner of my eye. His words didn't make me feel any safer in the castle, and I had the urge to move away from him.

"When did I ever say I was your friend?" he shot back, making me drop his arm and turn in place.

Crossing my arms over my chest, I settled him with a steely look. "You didn't.

I was assuming, but since you just pretty much said I couldn't trust anything you or anyone else in this place says, I'm figuring I'm wrong."

Asher made a clucking noise with his tongue and laced his fingers in front of him as he stepped closer to me. "I didn't say you couldn't trust me, and I would like to be your friend. God knows they are hard to come by in this place, but I wanted you to realize what you are up against. This isn't just some party where you will win a fairy tale ever-after at the end."

"I got that much, but back there, everyone seemed a bit more invested in their scores than I was, and I'm getting a bit tired of being in the dark."

He gave me a sympathetic look before taking my hands. "You did something none of those other idiots has ever accomplished. A nine out of ten, and a red score to boot. This doesn't just put you high in the running. It puts a target on your back. Everyone will be rooting for you to fail and will help it along if they can."

"But what does the red score even mean?" I asked. "Violet said her pink score had something to do with her looks? And the yellow one meant they thought you were annoying." I smiled, remembering how irritated Zara had been. "What does mine mean?"

"It means you're being considered as a convert."

Chapter 9

ASHER LEFT ME AT my bedroom door with one last piece of advice.

"Make friends." He locked eyes with me, gripping my shoulders firmly.

I let out a short laugh. "That's what Marsha said."

"Marsha's a smart boy, and if you follow his advice, you will make it through this."

I sighed and shook my arms. "I'd have a better chance of surviving if I had to pick crops or slaughter a cow, than making friends."

"Well," Asher chuckled, "as amusing as that would be to see, that's not what they will be looking for. Now, go get some sleep. Tomorrow is the interview portion, and you are going to need to look good enough to negate any fumbling you are bound to have."

Pursing my lips in displeasure, I left my sponsor there in the hallway. Where he went next, I didn't care. The only thing in my sights was my bed.

I fought my way out of my dress, leaving it lying on the floor as I climbed into the cool sheets. I didn't bother putting on night clothes though I did pull the comforter around my naked body and fell into a deep sleep.

Hoping not to dream after a long and stressful day was as useless as trying to sow a seed in a desert. While I couldn't express myself clearly in real life, my mind did a good job for me. I shouted at my stepmother for putting me in this situation, but she morphed into Zara with her razor-sharp nails and clawed at my face. The blood dripped from the wounds, and Asher and Marsha were there to clean them up with their tongues. I tried to push them away, but they held me down.

"We're your friends, Clarabelle. Let us help you," Marsha urged as he held one of my arms down. I whimpered as they lapped at my face until suddenly they were gone. I opened my eyes and found myself in the dark.

A single candle flickered to life, and I started toward it. When I reached the edge of the light, I saw the hand that had lit the candle. My eyes followed it up to meet that of Patrick Blordril. Cool eyes crinkled at the sides as he smiled at me. I found myself reaching for him though I still didn't know if I could trust him or not.

The leader of the Fold took me into his arm, and I pressed my ear against his chest. Where there should have been a heartbeat, there was none. Nothing, just an empty hollow for a chest.

I jerked away from him my brow furrowed in confusion, but he simply smiled fondly. His hand brushed the side of my face, and he leaned down as if to kiss me. But even as my eyes fluttered close to meet him, he bypassed my face and shouted in my ear, "Wake up, Clarabelle! It's another wonderful day!"

Ripped from my dream, I shot up in bed to find Daphne at my side. Her hair was no longer piled on top of her head, instead braided into three separate parts each part a different shade of pink. I wondered briefly if she did her own hair or if she had a sponsor of her own.

"Where's Asher?" I croaked as I clutched the covers to my chest. Suddenly, going to bed nude didn't seem like such a good idea.

"Oh, he'll be along shortly." She waved a perfectly manicured hand. "I'm just making the rounds, making sure all the guests get breakfast, and such."

"But there are so many of us. Don't you have someone to help you?" I stood from the bed taking the sheet with me over to where someone had laid out a plain shift dress. Picking it up, I frowned. Didn't anyone ever wear pants here?

Daphne snorted. "Usually, I only have twelve guests to attend to, but this year ... well." She sighed a bit irritably. "This year is different."

"Because Patrick Blordril is picking a convert, right?" I asked, slipping the dress over my head. When I could see again, I saw the astonished look on Daphne's face. "What?"

"Who told you that?" her voice had taken a low, hushed tone.

"Told me what?"

Daphne hurried to my side with a sense of urgency. "That Patrick Blordril was looking for a convert?"

Asher had been the one to tell me, but I didn't want to get him in trouble if he was trying to help me out. So instead of telling the truth, I shrugged. "I just heard it around."

Daphne stared at me for a moment longer, probably trying to decide if she believed me or not. Then her dazzling smile covered her face once more. "Well, no matter. I'm sure someone would have told you, eventually."

Doubtful. Highly doubtful.

"Nevertheless, we must push on." Daphne handed me my shoes and then turned to the door. "There is a schedule to keep, and you will want to have a full stomach for the interview portion. It's going to be just fabulous!"

She disappeared out my door, probably headed toward another guest's room to wake them up with her shrieking. I ran a hand over my face and came back with leftover makeup from yesterday. Grimacing at the disgusting feeling, I headed to the bathroom.

The shower in there was nothing like I had back home in the Glade, or even at my stepmother's. For one, it seemed to have infinite hot water. Usually, I was lucky to get a ten-minute warm shower before my stepsisters started theirs, turning the water ice cold. Secondly, several buttons lined the wall next to the handle. Curious by their purpose, I pushed one and then yelped when a jet of water shot out and hit me in the backside. I quickly pushed the button again, turning the jet off. I ignored the temptation to try the other buttons and finished my shower instead.

I toweled off and slipped the dress back over my head. I left my hair down to hang dry as I came out of the bathroom and into the now-occupied bedroom.

"She's here!" Neeka, one of Asher's companions, cried out.

The two other women turned from a table covered in fruits and cheeses, each of their faces lighting up in delight. Before I could prepare, they rushed to my side, each of them talking at once.

"Congratulations! I can't believe you got such a high score. And on the first day."

Willow patted me on the back with a familiar hand.

"I know, right?" Neeka responded with a nod of her head. "You are the only thing anyone in the castle can talk about, and yesterday was only the first day!"

"It's no surprise really," Rosel butted in. "Asher is her sponsor after all. No way anyone under him would score anything less than the best."

The other two nodded in agreement and then turned to me, finally quiet and waiting for my reply.

"He did a great job. I owe it all to him," I replied without much prompting. These women seemed to be easily appeased with compliments to Asher. I wished the rest of the guests were so easy to please.

"Speaking of Asher," I continued a moment later, "Where is he? I thought he was going to help me prepare for the interview?"

"Oh, he is!" Neeka answered. "We're to get your hair and makeup done while he puts the finishing touches on your outfit."

The way she said it made me wonder what needed finishing on whatever monstrosity Asher had planned for me.

While his clothing choices were lovely, definitely better than any of my stepmother's designs, I was more of a pants-and-shirt kind of girl and wearing all these frilly frocks made me uncomfortable in my own skin.

The trio went to work on making me look presentable while chatting about the latest gossip in the castle. It seemed not everyone agreed on the number of guests this year. Some thought it should have been like always. There shouldn't have been extra constituents just because certain people desired more choices. It wasn't fair to the servants who had to work overtime to keep us all fed.

I listened to them complain with intent interest. They seemed to forget that I was one of the guests when they were working as if I weren't even there. Which worked in my favor since no one else seemed to want to let us know what was going on.

"There!" Willow finally announced. "You are ready for Asher."

Glancing in the mirror, my eyes widened. They had braided my hair along the side of my head so that it fell over my shoulder and had inserted little flowers along each fold.

My eyelids were lined in pale pink, sprinkled with small glittering flakes, drawing attention to my dark eyes. I turned to the trio in awe.

"It's wonderful. Thank you." I smiled at them.

Collectively, they exchanged a pleased look before making a few minor adjustments. Then they started for the door. Before they could leave, I called out to them.

"What's it like to be a companion?"

The trio paused and once more exchanged a look before Willow came forward. "What you really want to ask is if we were chosen at an Election, which we were," she added before I could confirm or deny. "And I can't speak for all of us, but it was the best thing that ever happened to me."

I frowned at her explanation. "But what does being a companion mean? Do you ... you know ... with Asher?" I couldn't get the words out, my face heating up.

Willow laughed and the other two joined in. "No, no. It's not like that. While some of them do, Asher's not interested in sex. He's an artist. Clothes are the only thing he loves." There was a hint of sadness in her voice that I couldn't bring myself to ask about.

Instead, I nodded. "Thank you for telling me."

"No problem," Willow replied with a slight smile. "Now, Asher will be here briefly. Don't mess with your face or hair until then. Got it?" She shook a stern finger at me. "We don't want to have to redo all our hard work."

I agreed and then turned away as they left. So, they weren't collecting us to be sex slaves. That was good to know. But what was the point? Were they just lonely up here in their castle? I found that hard to believe.

Lost in my thoughts, I didn't hear Asher come in until he was reflected in the mirror beside me. Jumping in my seat, I clutched a hand to my heart. "Don't do that!"

"My apologies," Asher chuckled and then surveyed my hair and face. "My girls did a wonderful job. Just the touch needed to make this outfit the best yet."

I turned in my seat to see the dress Asher had brought in with him. Lying across my bed in a pile of pink lay the most beautiful thing I had ever seen. I got to my feet so I could get a better look at it.

I'd expected another dress, but this time, Asher had provided a two-part ensemble. The top was sleeveless with a high collar. It came to the waist where it billowed out in a cape-like fashion letting the dark brown pants beneath it show through. The only part I was a bit skeptical about was the triangle cut in the middle of the bodice. When I put it on, it would show far more cleavage than I had ever shown in my life.

"I thought we might compromise," Asher said from behind me. "Something a bit more flexible in movement but still with a dash of flair." He bent down and picked up something, then held it out to me, a pair of boots a darker shade of brown than the pants. "These only have a slight heel, so no more losing your shoes, got it?"

I blushed but took the shoes from him with a smile. "Thank you, this is great. Really."

As Asher helped me into the outfit, he went over what would happen today. "Not only are you trying to attract them with your clothing, but you will be asked all manner of questions to let them gauge what kind of person you are."

"Did you ask the girls those questions?"

My question seemed to startle him and then his lips tipped up. "Not as many as they will be asking you, but yes. I was happy to find them."

"They seem happy too," I commented as I adjusted the top to try to hide some of my breasts, but it was no use. The top fit like a glove and no amount of fighting it would lessen the effect Asher had wanted.

"Yes," Asher mused. "We are all quite lucky."

"Do you think I will be?" I asked through the mirror. "Happy, that is?"

Asher fluffed up the train of the shirt before coming around to face me. "Your happiness is up to you. You can't rely on anyone else to make it happen. But if you get the position I suggested you aim for, then yes. You will be quite happy."

He pestered over me a few minutes more before he announced I was ready. The result was stunning. I'd thought what he had put me in yesterday was daring. Today's put it to shame. While the top made me look girlish, the cleavage shown reminded them I was still a woman. The top contrasted with the bottom which screamed, 'I'm feminine but still tough.'

"Asher, you are a miracle worker." I grinned at him, not able to stop touching my new outfit.

"I know." He shrugged. "Now, let's go in there and show them what we are made of, ya?"

The guests were brought to the same room where we had read the board yesterday. Food was again laid out on the long table, and everyone was preoccupied with one thing or another. I quickly found Marsha and the others and headed toward them.

"Wow." Marsha stood as I approached. "You look great." His eyes darted down to my chest and his face heated before he glanced away.

"Thanks, Asher's great." I tried not to let my own blush show. I knew this top was going to get me more attention than I wanted. Even now, Narq stared blatantly at the open part and I had the urge to turn around.

"You look really pretty," Tillie commented dreamily.

I smiled softly at her and then glanced over her outfit. Her sponsor had gone for sexy this time, dressing her in a form-fitting yellow dress with thin straps and a daring split down the side. "You look great too."

Before we could talk anymore, Daphne came in and started calling out names. Each person came forward and left the room. They were gone for a long time before she came back again, calling out more names. This continued until the numbers began to dwindle.

Anxiety took away anyone's desire to talk, and barely anyone ate anything from the table. We seemed too nervous to hold anything down. I was suddenly glad I'd eaten plenty this morning, my stomach wouldn't be able to handle anything now.

Zara's name was called next, and she strode across the room, not even glancing my way. It seemed her sponsor hadn't gotten the memo that the leather look hadn't worked for her before, and I doubted it would work for her now.

Finally, Daphne called my name.

A lump rose in my throat, and I made my way over to her, my knees shaky. She led me out of the room and across the hall where she stopped at the double doors from which we had begun our parade yesterday.

"Now, just answer the questions as best you can. There are no right or wrong ones." Daphne patted me on the shoulder with a reassuring smile. "You're going to do great."

I didn't return her smile. As she gave me a little shove through the door, she announced, "Clarabelle Feldman."

Forcing my hands down to my sides, I made my way through the room where The Fold sat behind a long table once more. This time, instead of a taped x marking where I should stand, there was a chair. I sat down, thankful for it. If I had to stand there the whole time, I might have fainted.

"Feldman," a woman with bright red hair and long dangling earrings said. "I know that name."

"Yes," I said my voice coming out scratchy. I cleared my throat and tried again. "My father is the overseer of the southern part of the Glade."

The woman's face scrunched up in confusion. "Then what in the world are you doing here?"

I shrugged. "You tell me. You invited me."

This caused the other members to laugh. I kept my eyes on the others and away from the ones I really wanted to see. They bore into me as they asked me question after question. How old I was? Did I have siblings? Things they should have already known.

Then, when I thought it was finally over, Patrick Blordril spoke. "What do you like to do for fun?"

I frowned at his question. We didn't have much time for fun in the Glade. Or the means for it. Even moving to the Inner Circle I'd had a hard time finding something to fill my time which didn't seem trivial.

"It's not a hard question," he said a moment later when I didn't respond. "Do you like to read?"

"No," I said, partly glad he was helping me along. "I don't see the point of books."

"Why not?" he asked, bringing a hand to his face as he studied me. "Don't you want to just run away to a fantasy world every once in a while?"

I shook my head. "I live in the real world. A fantasy world is only good to me if it's being used to start a fire."

"What about history?" he offered next. "Are you not interested in knowing about the past?"

I frowned. "What's the point? Today is what matters. Nothing that happened to someone else can help me put food on my table or a roof over my head."

Patrick leaned back in his chair and seemed to think for a moment. "Those things are important to you, yes?"

I half laughed. "Aren't they to everyone?"

"Most people, when asked what's important, would answer with 'looks' or 'money'."

"I'm not most people," I retorted, becoming a bit irritated.

"We can see that." He smirked, and his companions laughed.

"What I can't see is the point to all of this," I snapped. "You bring us here, lavish us with food and fancy clothing," - I jerked at the bottom of my shirt - "when you have people starving out in the rest of the rings."

The entire table became silent. Patrick's pale eyes locked onto me with such intensity that I was sure he would have me killed for my outburst. But he simply waved

Daphne forward. She rushed to my side and led me out of the room.

Once in the hallway, I collapsed against the wall. I hadn't meant to get so upset, but I couldn't just sit there and talk about such nonsense when they were clearly blind to what was going on in the rest of Alban.

"I'm dead," I muttered to myself. "They're going to kill me."

"Nonsense." Daphne waved me off. "They've never killed anyone for speaking their mind, and quite frankly, I applaud you for your bravery. They need someone to bring them down a peg or two."

I stared up at her, my heart racing. "Really? You think so?"

"I know so." She gave me a reassuring smile. "Now, let's get some food in that belly. I know that you must be famished."

While my stomach growled in response, I didn't think I could eat anything until I knew for sure I'd be alive tomorrow. Or worst yet if my family would be.

Chapter 10

AFTER OUR INTERVIEWS, WE weren't sent back to the gathering room. Instead, we were given free rein to do with our time what we liked until the party that evening. I spent that time pacing my room, wringing my hands in front of me.

While Daphne had reassured me that I wouldn't be punished for my little outburst, I wasn't so sure. The longer I was left to my own devices, the more anxious I became. No other guest would have dared shout at them the way I had. If I was in their position, I knew I wouldn't let me live.

But what I wanted to know was why it was taking so long for them to come get me.

The television screen on my bedroom wall came on by itself, and a song played before the scoreboard from before showed on the screen. I didn't want to look. I didn't dare look. My score yesterday had been great, but then again, my little bout with my shoes looked like a cute mishap compared to today's disaster.

Unfortunately, the screen didn't turn off, and I couldn't figure out how to turn it off on my own. So, to stave off the urge to check it, I marched from my room. The door slammed shut behind me making me wince and search the hallway, but no one noticed.

Arms wrapped around my waist, I strolled through the hallway with no destination in mind. I just couldn't stay in that room any longer, and they had said we could do what we wanted. If I was going to die today, I wanted to go outside at least one more time.

I searched for a way to get outdoors, like a garden or a terrace, but with no luck. Tired of looking, I sank down against the wall and buried my head in my lap. Why couldn't I have stayed in the Glade? If my father hadn't married Belinda, Julianna would be the one here, and I'd be back home clearing the crops for the new season.

My eyes pricked with tears and I didn't fight them. My shoulders heaved as I wallowed in my misery, not caring if anyone saw me. I was dead anyway. What did I care what they thought?

Like everything that had happened to me since I arrived, I didn't have much choice in the matter. My solace was broken by a tut-tutting and then a hand on my shoulder. I slowly glanced up from my lap and saw the older woman from before.

Venna.

"Dear, why are you crying?" she asked in a motherly tone. I found myself wanting to throw myself into her arms and bury my face in her chest, the same kind of thing I would have done to my own mother, but I refrained. I didn't know this woman, and I highly doubted she would let a stranger impose upon her in such a manner.

I wiped my nose with the back of my hand not caring that I probably look a blotchy mess. "I wanted to go outside."

My voice was small and childlike, making Venna smile. "Well, why didn't you just ask? You can get lost in the place."

She helped me to my feet, and I chuckled. "They should give us a map or something."

"There is one, in your room."

"Oh." I frowned at her words and realized I had been so caught up in my own misery I hadn't bothered to check out what my room had to offer me. The only thing that had seemed important had been staying alive and finding a map hadn't been part of that.

Venna patted my hand and guided me down the hallway. "But since you are here, I'd be happy to take you to the garden. You are quite close, actually."

My body sagged in relief. Soon, I'd be outside. Everything would be alright as soon as I got out of here.

"You know," Venna started, "I knew from the start you were special."

"How so?" I glanced at her from the side. "You don't even know me."

"Because you didn't come in wearing your finest or hide how lost you were." She spoke as though it were the best compliment she could give me. Which, as far as I knew, it might have been.

"Fat lot of good it's done me." I snorted.

"Nonsense." She clicked her tongue at me. "You've had the highest score two days in a row. I'd say it has done you well."

"What?" I gaped at her. "I had a high score again?"

This time it was her turn to frown. "Didn't you read the scores? You and that girl ... what's her name? The little one with the pretty eyes?"

"Violet."

"Yes." She nodded. "Her. You two are almost neck and neck. Though, her color is still pink. I can't blame them though. Her eyes really are something unusual."

I wasn't really listening to her anymore, too stunned by what she had told me. How the hell had I gotten a high score again? I'd been as stiff as a statue and hadn't proved to be any more interesting than a fly on a horse's backside. I had been so sure I'd be killed or sent home before the party even happened.

Venna stopped us at a set of glass double doors. "Well, I'm sure you will do great. Many of us are rooting for you!"

Smiling, I nodded but with the outdoors being so close to me, I couldn't really find the initiative to continue the conversation.

Instead, I thanked her and exited through one of the doors.

Instantly, the sun warmed my face, and I took a deep breath. The air wasn't as clean as it was in the Glade, but it was better than nothing. Enough that I almost fell asleep standing there against the palace doors.

Eventually, I opened my eyes and took in the world around me. The garden wasn't like my mother's back home. There weren't any fruits or vegetables growing, just long rows of different colored flowers. I moved away from the doors and walked down the rows, taking in the brilliant colors, though sadly they were just as manufactured as the ones in the Inner Circle. Did nothing truly grow here?

As I strolled through the garden, I nodded at a few guests who had also come outside to enjoy the day, but for the most part, I kept to myself. About half an hour too late, I realized I should have been making friends with them rather than pretending they weren't there. Too caught up in my own misery, I had forgotten all about Martha and Asher's advice.

I turned on my heel to catch up with the couple who had walked by me but was caught by a servant. The young woman handed me an envelope before darting away without a word.

Turning it over in my hand, I didn't see a seal from the Fold, but it did have my name on it. I glanced around me and then found a bench to sit on. Opening the envelope, I held my breath as I read the note.

My dearest Clarabelle,

Your stepmother has fallen deeply ill, and she calls for you to come to her side. We miss you and wish to have you home again with us. Please come before it is too late.

Love, your father.

Frowning at the note, I didn't know what to make of it. It wasn't from him. He never called me Clarabelle, even when he was mad at me. Another sign was the reason he wanted me to come home. If Belinda were sick, she wouldn't have asked for me. I'd be the last person on this earth she'd want to see on her deathbed. So, the letter had to be a trick.

But who had sent it?

I got to my feet just in time to see Zara and the two girls she had been ranting to last night, watching me from behind a tree. They giggled and hid when they realized they had been spotted.

There was the culprit.

I sighed and started for the palace, not bothering to confront her. Asher had said she might try something. Even Marsha had. But of all the things she could have done, a fake letter from home seemed a bit childish.

Crumpling the letter in my hand, I made my way back to my room. Thankfully, I only got lost once before I found my door, its condition a little different from how I'd left it.

Painted across the off-white wood, in what could have been lipstick, was an array of insults. Slut. Whore. Cheater. Someone had even gone so far as to write 'Moo' on there. As if being compared to a cow wasn't something I had heard before.

Sighing, I entered my room. There wasn't anything I could do about it. I'd been targeted as the person to beat, and now they were trying to use grade-school antics to scare me away. But their tricks had the opposite effect on me.

Now that I knew being different from the others wasn't a hindrance but rather what might help me win, I would be as different as I could be. No more trying to fit in with them and their Soft Hand minds. I was from the Glade, and I would act like it.

If Patrick or any of the others wanted me after that, then more the better. Now, to figure out how.

Chapter 11

ASHER AND HIS TEAM showed up to my room shortly after my epiphany. The trio took one look at my tear-stained face and huddled around me trying to find out what was wrong.

"You scored big again!" Neeka shouted. "Why aren't you dancing around the room in your knickers? I know I would be."

I gave her a small smile. "Probably because I was too worried about getting killed to check the scoreboard."

"What?" Asher cried out, coming to my side. "What happened? Did someone try to hurt you?"

I shook my head and then explained what happened in the interviews. Their reaction wasn't to gasp in horror but instead to laugh hysterically. It was my turn to be concerned.

Asher finished laughing and cleared his throat before taking me by the arms. "They might be a lot of things, but being so petty as to punish someone for telling the truth has never been one of them. Many of them probably had no idea what you were talking about and found your outburst amusing. Which would be reason enough for your high score. But I think it's more than that."

"What else could it be?" I glanced around me. "I mean, I'm thankful I'm not dead, and I'm flattered they would give me such a high score. One that owes a lot of thanks to you and your outfit." I gestured down at my clothes. "But why else would I get a high score?"

Asher exchanged a look with the trio before he said, "A few reasons. They either see you as a threat. Or they want you desperately." The trio giggled at the last bit, earning them a glare from me.

The thought of anyone wanting me desperately, or any other way, was a bit strange to me. I was just the overseer's daughter; no one wanted me. Except maybe the overseer. But he was my father. He had to love me.

"So, what's the outfit look like tonight?" I asked, ready to get the conversation off me and my outrageous score.

The trio and Asher exchanged a pleased look before they pulled out three suitcases. Frowning at the bags, I glanced back at my team. "What's all this?"

"Well," Neeka started grinning like a fiend.

"It's your outfits." Willow smirked, and then Rosel added, "For the balls."

My mouth dropped open and then I stuttered, "Balls? Like plural?"

The trio nodded enthusiastically.

"Wait, just a second." I waved my hands in front of me. "I was told of one party. One." I held up a single finger, shoving it in their faces.

"And that had been the plan," Asher explained, his hands tucked in his pockets. "Until they realized how many guests there were this year ... that it would be ridiculously hard to pick without weeding out the others."

"So ..." I drew out, pointing to the bags. "I'm assuming there are three balls?"

"Yes!" the trio cried out and then started to unveil their goods.

"Hold on." Asher stopped them. He pressed his finger against his lips as he glanced over them before he pointed to the one in Willow's hands. "That one. Only show her that one."

"Why?" I asked turning to him. "What does it matter if I see them all? I'm going to have to wear them after all."

Asher smiled and held his hands out. "Humor me."

Growling, I dragged a hand through my hair. "Fine. Let's get this over with. I've got a ball to get to."

Neeka and Rosel slumped slightly, their excitement deflated by Asher's commands. Willow, on the other hand, started to unwrap her goods, her eyes full of eagerness.

"This one is my favorite," Willow told me as she uncloaked a mint-green gown. Full-skirted with small butterflies decorating the gauze material, the dress was strapless and came with long matching elbow length gloves.

"Wow." I gaped. "It's like right out of a fairytale."

"I thought you didn't read?" Asher asked, making me eyeball him.

"How do you know about that?" He hadn't been in the interview process.

Ashe crossed his arms over his chest with a mysterious grin. "People talk. Even the members of the Fold."

Not really believing him, I dropped the subject and turned to the trio. "Alright, let's get this over with. I've got a party to get to."

The three women crowded around me with equally creepy grins. I realized then that what they had done to me before had been child's play and the real challenge would be tonight's party and the following two. If the Fold didn't pick me for a position, they would be sure to remember me for my style.

Three hours later and I was ready. Asher and the trio had outdone themselves this time, and I had a feeling it was just the beginning. I stared longingly at the other two covered outfits wondering if they were even better than the one on my body now.

"Time to go, princess." Asher offered me an arm with a grin. "Can't leave your audience waiting."

I made a disbelieving sound in the back of my throat before sliding my arm into his. "The only thing they will be waiting for is me to fall flat on my face."

Asher rolled his eyes. "You're wearing flats. The only way you are going to fall is if you get too drunk to walk."

"That's not going to happen," I pointed out as we walked down the hall. Asher had outdone himself. The dress felt light as air, so it seemed like I was floating each time I moved. If this outfit didn't get me the convert position, I didn't know what else would.

"So, what should I expect at this thing?" I asked as we neared the ballroom. After Veena's information, I'd finally taken the time to look at the map of the palace. The extent of the map had been impressive. They even had a dungeon. At the time, I had shuddered at the thought of what might happen down there. When I'd asked Asher about it, he'd simply said it was more of a storage unit than a torture chamber.

"Torture for your nose maybe," he'd said, laughing.

Now, as he walked me to the first of three events, he wasn't laughing. His eyes faced forward, and a sort of seriousness marred his usually teasing expression.

"You will need to be careful," he started, his grip on my hand tightening. "The Fold might want you, but that means the others will hate you even more."

"What can they do though?" I shrugged. "It's not like they could kill me right there on the dance floor. Wait." I pulled us to a stop. "There is dancing, right?"

"Of course."

I chewed on my bottom lip not letting Asher lead me any further. "That might be a problem."

"Don't tell me you can't dance?" He quirked a brow and then laughed as my face heated. "It's not that hard. If anyone asks, just follow their lead. Let the music guide you through the steps."

"If you say so," I muttered, starting down the hall once more. "But if I faceplant, then I'm blaming you."

"You won't." Asher chuckled and stopped at a set of closed double doors. Music came through the walls, and my heart began to race. This was really happening. Everything would be decided, starting tonight.

I stared at the door not really seeing it. My fingers were turning white from how tightly I held onto Asher's arm. If it bothered my sponsor, he didn't complain.

"You'll be fine." He patted my hand and unwound me from his arm. "Just be your usual charming self, and everything will be fine."

Nodding my head, I reached for the door handle. I took a deep breath in and let it out as I pulled on the door. The music increased in volume, and I shut the door.

"I can't do this." I turned to Asher my eyes wide with panic. "If I go in there, that means they are going to be picking the positions and ... and I don't know what I want."

Asher sighed and grabbed my hands in his. Bringing them up to his mouth, he placed a kiss on the back of them. "Of all the guests I've had the pleasure of sponsoring, you are by far my favorite. I've told you more than I've ever told any guest before." He paused for a moment, something dark passing over his eyes before he said, "I won't lie to you, there are things at work which the people outside of the Core don't know about, things that need to change, and I knew the moment I saw you in the Inner Circle that you could make that happen."

I frowned at his words, not quite understanding what he was talking about. And then it hit me. "You put my name on the list, didn't you?"

He didn't deny it but kept his eyes on me. "You will be the convert and not just any." He shook his head. "*The* convert. At Patrick's side, you will have access to all kinds of things those from the Glade would never dream of. You'll be able to make a difference. Not just for you, but for everyone in Alban. But first," - he turned me around to face the double doors once more - "you have to go in."

I didn't have a chance to ask him anymore because the doors opened from the inside and Asher took advantage of the moment to shove me inside. The whole room stared at me as I stood frozen in place by the doors. A mixture of feelings was directed my way, some of awe, no doubt for the beautiful gown I wore, others disinterested, but several of disdain. Maybe even hate. Zara's eyes held something malicious.

Swallowing hard, I moved away from the doors and toward the table of food that had been laid out. If I was going to get through this, I was going to need a drink.

Picking up a plate, I grabbed random things from the table not really paying much mind. If I looked like I was eating, no one would ask me to dance, or at least, I hoped. As I came to the end of the table, I picked up a glass of dark red liquid. Giving it a sniff, the scent of it burned my nose.

Alcohol. Perfect.

Taking my treasures with me, I made my way around the room. I hadn't seen Marsha or the others yet, but they were bound to be here somewhere. I sat down at an empty table along the edges of the dance floor and scanning the ballroom. The thirty-six guests were all here but mixed in were the members of the Fold. The woman from the interview who had questioned why I was even here was chatting up Narq. For a moment, I wondered where Patrick could be. Was he out in the crowd somewhere? He wasn't on the dance floor.

I chugged my drink as I chastised myself for caring. *He's the symbol of everything you hate. The reason your family and friends live in poverty while his little pets fatten themselves up every day.*

Even as I tried to convince myself otherwise, I couldn't help searching for his white head of hair. After minutes of looking, I almost thought he hadn't shown up, but then I caught a flash of white that disappeared out the balcony doors.

I got to my feet, intent on finding him and getting this whole thing over with, but a figure blocked my way.

"There you are, the girl from the Glade." A man stood in front of me, of average height with unmemorable features ... except when he smiled, his teeth were sharper than most, making his smile look vicious instead of endearing.

"You found me," I replied with a forced smile. "What can I do for you?"

The man took my hand in his and brought it up to his mouth, I had a half moment where I thought he might bite me before he skimmed his mouth over the back of my hand. "I just wanted to introduce myself to the high scorer of the Election. I'm Beaford, the treasurer and second adviser to our esteemed leader, Patrick Blordril."

I took my hand back as soon as I was able, the urge to wipe it off overwhelming, even with the glove. "I'd introduce myself, but I believe you know all there is to know about me."

Beaford laughed. "Hardly. I'm sure there are quite a few things I would love to get to know about you." He inched closer, lowering his voice to what would normally be used for a lover.

Swallowing hard, I took a step back, my gaze skating across the room for a distraction. Thankfully Marsha caught my eye. He waved to me, and I gave a small wave in return before turning to Beaford. "I apologize. It looks like I'm being flagged down. Maybe we'll talk again later?"

I didn't give him the chance to answer before my feet led me away from him to Marsha who stood with Tillie and Violet. We said the usual pleasantries about each other's outfits before the conversation turned to the elephant in the room.

"Don't you find it odd?" Violet asked, fiddling with her glass of dark liquid.

"What?" Marsha responded, his eyes searching around the room as if to find what she spoke of.

"After all the parading around and the scores, that now we are just hanging out." She gestured around the room. "Just expected to spend time with them like we're friends and not ants beside giants."

I knew there was a reason I liked her. Thinking about her words, I didn't even look up when someone handed me another glass. It wasn't until I began to bring it to my lips and Narq's hand shot out of nowhere did I question it.

"I wouldn't drink that if I were you." He took the glass from my hand and dumped it in a nearby plant. The plant began to hiss, and smoke rose from it, the leaves turning brown.

"What the hell was that?" Violet cried out, horror on her face. I wanted to know the answer as well, but I had a feeling I already knew.

"Losers never play fair," Tillie said mysteriously from her spot. Her eyes were focused on a group of girls among which I immediately recognized Zara's dark head.

I lifted my skirt, intent on confronting her but a commotion from the other side of the room stopped me. Another girl, a bit older than me with auburn hair, clutched her throat as her skin began to disintegrate around it. She fell to the floor as people gasped and screamed in terror.

My heart raced as I realized that could have been me. If Narq hadn't been there to stop me, I'd be the one writhing on the floor, my skin melting off. Suddenly, I wasn't in the party-going mood.

I turned on my heel, away from the girl who was most certainly dead now, and back toward the doors. Brushing past Narq, I nodded. "Thank you."

"Anytime." He gave me a two-finger salute before his attention turned back to the gathering crowd of Fold members. "Too bad, she really had a chance. A seven and a red. I guess that means you and Violet need to watch your back." He shot me a cocky grin that I didn't understand.

No longer caring about Asher's plans, or about finding Patrick, I spun around and searched for the exit. I did not sign up for this. Any of it.

Chapter 12

I DIDN'T SLEEP AT all that night, jumping at every little sound. Asher had gone off to wherever he went when he wasn't dressing me and hadn't been back for me to tell him about last night's festivities and how I almost died.

A plate of food waited for me as I came out of the shower, but I couldn't eat. I stared out the window for a long time, trying to decipher what had happened.

How could someone do something so vicious? All for what? Some position? But if what Asher had said, being Patrick's convert would mean more than just having riches; it would mean power too. Power to change things.

The screen in my room powered on, and an anthem played before the board I'd come to loath flickered on. I told myself I wouldn't look. I didn't care about how I did or whatever one else thought, but I found myself in front of the screen without even knowing I had moved.

This time the scoreboard had changed. Instead of numbers beside each guest's name, there were only colors highlighting them. There was no legend to tell me what they meant, but I glanced over at the table where my food tray sat and saw a piece of paper.

Grabbing it, I tried to match up the colors with the names on the board. Four were highlighted gray, which meant they were being placed as servants. One, a pale blue. A companion. Seven were struck out, meaning they were being sent home, their memories wiped. I wondered why the girl from last night had been grouped in with the seven. Surely, they weren't sending her home to her family like that?

The rest of the names weren't highlighted. Instead, they were all bundled together. Those were the ones who were left. Only twenty-four of us left, and I didn't need a legend to tell me who was in the lead. The name at the top of the list, the bane of my existence, was still mine.

Violet's name sat right below and then a few I didn't recognize and then Marsha's. Zara's sat in eighth place with Narq at eleventh. At least he was safe from Zara's wrath. Too bad for those of us above her though.

I didn't get to be alone for long because the trio came bursting through my door. The moment they saw me, they started to cry, each one of them clinging to me as though their lives depended on it.

"Oh, Clarabelle," Neeka cried, her makeup streaking from her tears. "How horrible it must have been for you. I hear that girl's death was positively gruesome."

"It wasn't pretty, that's for sure." I grimaced as the image of the poor girl clutching her neck in agony.

Willow made a displeased sound. "How can you make light of such a tragedy?"

I shrugged. "I'm not but running screaming down the halls won't really help the situation."

"Logical, I agree." Rosel nodded, the most composed of the three.

"Besides," I continued, withdrawing myself from their clutches, "seeing her die wasn't half as bad as knowing it could have been me. Would have had Narq not saved me."

"What?" they screeched in unison.

"Do you know who did it?" Willow asked.

"You have to tell someone," Neeka urged, looking to her friends for support. They all nodded their heads in vigorous agreement.

I bit the end of my thumb for a second and then sighed. "I don't have proof. Only suspicions. And anyway, who would I tell?"

"Asher!" they said together.

"What could he do?" I asked, wrapping my arms around myself as I turned toward the window. "He's just my sponsor. Surely he doesn't have much pull in what goes on around here? Probably nothing more than a certifiable servant."

"I would hope not," Asher's voice called out from behind me. I spun around to see him standing by the trio, his hands behind his back and a perturbed expression on his face.

My own face heated with embarrassment. "I'm sorry. I wasn't trying to be insulting. I'm just flustered by everything." I waved a hand in the air, hoping to make what I'd said seem less important.

"I understand," Asher said carefully. "You've just seen something horrific, something that I warned you might happen. You were lucky that boy stopped you in time or I wouldn't have a guest to sponsor."

"I know, Asher." I shook my head, hoping I looked as remorseful as I felt. "I should have been more careful."

"Yes, you should have," he snapped, the first sign of anger in his gaze. At my startled expression, he sighed and ran a hand over his face. "I was like you once."

"Freaked out?" I asked.

"No. A guest." He smiled when I gasped. "Then I played the game and became a convert to one of the most powerful members of the Crimson Fold. Now, look where I am." He gestured elaborately. "A sponsor with companions of my own. I get to do what I want, when I want. But you know what got me here?" he raised a brow.

"Your winning personality?" I guessed.

"No," he sniffed, adjusting his jacket over his shirt, "I made friends. The right friends. The kind with power."

I stared at him for a moment before a light went off in my head. "You don't mean making friends with the guests, do you?"

His lips ticked up, and he locked eyes with me before turning to the trio. "Why don't we make Clara look better than she feels right now?"

The trio didn't need to be told twice before they descended upon me. Today, I wasn't in the talkative mood, and I just let them do with me as they willed. They poked and prodded, yanking on my hair until it resembled some elegant twist I'd never be able to replicate.

When they finished, the circles under my eyes from lack of sleep were gone, and it was like I'd never been at death's door. This time the dress was a dark blue, with a skirt of taffeta. The sleeves and back were sheer and sparkled like stars. It definitely made me seem tougher than I felt.

"Great job, as usual, Asher." I smiled at him briefly through the three-way mirror, but my heart wasn't in it.

I hadn't forgotten what Asher wanted from me. What he had asked me to do. What I had to do.

It was one thing to be chosen as the convert without trying, it was completely another thing to purposely seek out the leader of Alban in the hopes of making friends.

Snorting at the thought, I ignored the questioning looks the trio gave me and headed for the door. I didn't wait for Asher to escort me this time. I wasn't in the chit-chatting mood, and I'd had about as much advice as I could handle for one lifetime.

My eyes were totally focused on getting to the ball when I bumped into a man in the hallway, I didn't realize who it was until he grabbed me by the arm. "Clara?"

I tried to jerk my arm away from the person, but then my mind registered the voice. Blinking, I stared up at someone who creepily enough resembled my father.

"Dad?" my voice came out a cautious whisper as my eyes darted down the hallway.

With no one there to see, I pulled him into the nearest room which happened to be an office. Whose office I didn't really know or care, not while my father was standing before me.

Hair mostly gray, only a few spots showed that he had once been as dark headed as me. His face seemed to have aged ten years since I had seen him last. He had kissed my forehead the way he always did before he left to go back to the Glade, when he had been wearing his usual work clothes. But now, he could have put Asher to shame in his finery.

"What are you doing here?" I gaped at him, not believing my eyes.

"I came to see you." He moved closer to me, his eyes taking in my clothes. A softness settled over his face. "You look beautiful, Clara. Just like your mother."

Embarrassment came over me, and I shifted uncomfortably. "It's just a bit of clothes and makeup. Nothing to make a fuss about."

"I just wish she could be here to see you now." He sighed and then stomped his foot and cursed. "Why couldn't you have waited until I came home? I thought I raised you better than to jump in feet first with these evil bastards?"

Irritation filled me at his accusations. "Apparently, your wife forgot to mention she was the one who had me sent here."

Surprise covered his face before acceptance took its place. "She will be dealt with. Right now, we have to get you out of here."

He reached for me, but I pulled away.

"Clara? What is it? You don't want to be, here do you?" His question held a hint of disbelief, and I shook my head.

"I didn't want this." I gestured around the room and then violently flipped my skirt. "Any of this. I was going to wait for you, but the jerks had a pin in the invitation. Blood bound, she said." I mocked Belinda's voice.

"So? Why does that matter?"

My brow furrowed as I stared him down. "Do you think they would go to the trouble of making an invitation that knows when I open it if they knew I could get away at any moment? Who knows what will happen to you or me" - I jerked a hand in his direction - "if I leave now?"

"We'll figure it out." My father grabbed my arms, a desperation in his hold. "We just have to get out of here first."

For a moment, I believed him. I let him lead me to the door before I stopped him again. Something didn't make sense.

"How did you even get in here? It's not like they would let you walk through the front door."

My father stared down at the ground the way he did when he'd done something he wasn't proud of. "I went to the mayor."

Those five words were all it took for me to yank my arm away from him. Zara. Of course, she'd be involved in this. Who knew what she promised if I left. It seemed she would do anything to make her way to the top, even give my father false hope in thinking I could get out of this alive.

"You were tricked," I muttered, avoiding his eyes. "They wouldn't let me leave even if I wanted to. No matter what the mayor promised you."

"No, no." He shook his head as if trying to convince him more than me. "They promised you'd be okay. That if I brought you home, took you out of the race, everything would be fine."

"Tell that to the girl they just murdered last night," I snapped. "No, I'm not going anywhere. She's gone too far. I'm not letting her win. Not now."

"But Clara," my father said, trying to stop me again, "you can't stay here. It's not safe. You don't know what these people will do to you. What they've done to plenty of others."

I scoffed. "So far, they've done nothing but put me in fancy clothes and ply me with food. What that psycho Zara has done though ..." I shook my head, the girl from last night's face in my mind once more. "Unforgivable."

Pushing past him, I exited the office and started back for the ballroom. I didn't turn to see if my father had left. He'd get back out the way he came in.

The only thing on my mind now was winning this thing. Or at least making sure Zara didn't. God knew we didn't need someone like her whispering in Patrick Blordril's ear.

Chapter 13

THE ROOM WENT QUIET for the second time when I threw the double doors open. Like a madwoman on a mission, which I was beginning to think I was, I strode through the room, my whole focus on finding Patrick and ending this thing for once and for all.

Unfortunately, he didn't seem to have the same plans as I did because I couldn't find him. What was with him? This was his party, and he couldn't find the time to even attend it?

Growling in frustration, I pushed through the crowd not worried about who I was offending, until one person grabbed me.

"Hey!" I tried to jerk away but when I saw who it was, I stopped. "Sorry, Marsha. I didn't mean to shove you like that."

"Don't worry about it." He smiled, the dimples in his cheeks showing through. "Honestly, I'm just glad to see you are okay. You took off pretty fast last night."

"Yeah, I was a bit freaked out." I flushed, my eyes going to the ground.

"We all were." Marsha placed his hand on my shoulder, giving it a squeeze. "I can't tell you how relieved I was to find your name on the scoreboard this morning. I thought for sure you weren't going to come."

"It's harder than that to get rid of me." My eyes caught a movement to my right, and my face closed down.

Zara.

For once, her sponsor had put her in something more girly and less evil incarnate. The pink frills didn't match the mixture of emotion on her face when she saw me. First surprise and then confusion and finally rage.

I waved with an over-exaggerated smile causing her to huff and stomp away. When I turned around laughing to myself, I came face to face with a wide-eyed Marsha.

Laughter cut off mid-laugh, I cleared my throat and ran a hand over the back of my neck. "Are you thirsty? I'm really thirsty. I think I'm going to get a drink. Excuse me."

When I tried to sidestep him, his hand shot out faster than I expected. Hand clasped in his he drew me closer, his voice going low. "What was that all about?"

My eyes darted around the room to the remaining guests and members of the Fold. Most of them hardly noticed our display, but a few people were starting to look our way. I tried to withdraw my hand slowly, but he held fast.

"It's complicated," I said between clenched teeth.

"Then explain it to me," he countered and then his eyes went to the dance floor. "Better yet, dance with me."

Before I could decline, he led me through the crowd and onto the dance floor. Thankfully, they were playing a slow song, or I'd have been completely lost. Even so, I wouldn't have been either way because Marsha seemed to be an expert dancer.

"You're good at this," I commented, holding onto his broad shoulders as he led me around the floor. "Where did a butcher boy learn to dance?"

Marsha smiled and threw his head back laughing. "We're not in the Glade, Clara. Everyone learns to dance in school."

"Not me," I muttered staring down at our feet. "We didn't have time to learn such things, too busy trying to stay alive."

My words caused Marsha to go silent. I peeked up at him to see him staring over my head, a closed-off look on his face. We went through the motions of the song for a moment before he finally spoke again.

"I understand things are different where you are from, but you can't hold it against me for being born where I was. I had as much choice as you did." His eyes locked with mine, showing the first sign of anger I'd ever seen in him.

"I'm sorry." I stared at his left shoulder not able to meet his eyes anymore. "I've been angry for so long it's just so easy to take it out on anyone not from the Glade. Which seems to be everyone now."

"And what of Zara? Is she the target of your anger?"

My head jerked up at the mention of Zara and my gaze narrowed. "No, that's something completely different."

"You know, Narq thinks she was the one who poisoned that girl last night. What do you think?" he asked, but before I could answer, the music stopped. We parted slightly and clapped for the band, and then another song started. One with more of an off-beat which meant I was out of my depth.

I tried to exit the dance floor, but Marsha caught my hand once more, bringing me back to him. I clutched onto him as he swung us around the floor in a happy jig, and by the end of it, I was laughing. For the first time since I moved to the Inner Circle, I felt a semblance of happiness.

"See?" Marsha said, slightly out of breath. "Not everything has to be life or death. You can just have fun dancing with no consequences."

Just then I felt eyes on me. I glanced around the room searching for the culprit behind the feeling. Then a hand tapped on my shoulder, and I froze.

Marsha stilled against me, and I knew before I turned who it would be.

"May I cut in?" Patrick's asked, his voice cool. It might have been a question, but the tone he used left no room for declining, which Marsha didn't even try. He gave me a slightly worried look before stepping away from me.

"Of course," he said with a small bow. "That's if it's okay with Clara."

I could have kissed him at that moment but knew I couldn't have told Patrick no. I had to make friends. What better way to make friends than an intimate dance, right?

"It's fine," I said, giving Marsha a reassuring smile before turning to Patrick. "I'd be happy to dance with the leader of our great country."

Patrick's lip turned up slightly, but he didn't call my bluff. Placing one hand on my hip and the other in my hand, he drew me to him. The dark color of his suit only offset the paleness of his eyes and hair, the contrast something otherworldly.

"How are you enjoying yourself, Clarabelle?" he asked, his eyes alight with mirth. "Staying out of trouble, I would hope?"

"Not as much as I would like," I countered. Taking a second to glance around the room I realized all eyes as well as several cameras were on us. How the hell would I make friends if I couldn't get a moment of peace?

"I heard about what happened last night," he commented after a moment.

"Yeah," I leaned back to meet his gaze, and before I could help it I snapped, "And where were you, our fearless leader?"

Patrick didn't get angry at my accusation. Instead, he sighed. "Unfortunately, I was called away. A fearless leader's work is never done, I'm afraid." He smiled slightly, making the skin around his eyes crinkle.

"Well, if you are going to throw a party, you should be at it."

He chuckled and squeezed my hand. "Why? Did you miss me?"

"Hardly," I scoffed, turning my eyes away from me. "Can't miss someone I don't know."

"Then do." My gaze shot back to his at his words, my brow scrunching up. "Get to know me that is. It's no secret, I have my eyes set on your as my convert, but I wouldn't want you to come to me without really getting to know me."

"Why?" I asked suspicion in my voice. "You could order me to be your convert, and I wouldn't be able to say no. Why do you care if I come willingly?"

Patrick leaned in close, "Now, would a friend do that?"

His words startled me enough to let him go and take a step back. Asher. It had to be. Were he and the leader of all of Alban in on this together?

Before I could ask any of the questions swirling around in my head, a sharp cry caught my ears. No one else seemed to notice, their ears full of the music, distracted and having a good time, but I did.

Without a word, I turned from Patrick and toward the sound. Several more sharp cries and then a whimper led me to the balcony. At the edge, hidden in the dark, stood three figures, while a fourth laid on the ground, likely the one who had cried out.

"You are nothing," Zara snarled and then she kicked the figure on the ground. Not thinking of my actions, I rushed over to the three and tackled Zara to the ground.

We struggled for dominance for a moment, turning over and over on the balcony floor. Her sharp nails scratched at my face and pain blossomed as I grabbed at her short hair. She howled and jabbed me in the side. I let go to defend myself from her hits. She used my distraction to flip us over, so she sat on top of me.

"Stupid dirty peasant," she screamed in my face as her fists came down on the arms I had braced in front of me. "You shouldn't be here. Why didn't you just leave when you had the chance?"

"Because I'm not a coward," I snapped back which made her pause in her assault long enough for me to get one good shot in. Blood spewed from her nose as she fell back. Shoving at her, I knocked her completely off me and crawled to my feet.

Her minions stood watching from the sidelines, not even moving an inch to help their leader. Behind them lay a groaning Violet, her face bloodied and bruised. I rushed to her side, only barely noticing that we had an audience.

"Violet!" I touched her gently, afraid to hurt her any more than she already was. "Can you hear me?"

Violet's gem-colored eyes peeked open, and she tried to sit up. But she cried out, her hand going to her side. I searched for whatever was hurting her but couldn't find a wound, or even any blood.

"She probably broke a rib," Patrick's voice said from behind me. "We'll need to get her to the infirmary quickly."

I turned to see him and a few others hovering in the doorway to the balcony, and thankfully also blocking the cameras from seeing this.

Kneeling by my side, he reached beneath her and slowly lifted her into his arms. I watched in awe as the leader of all of Alban did something he could have commanded another to do. Maybe I'd been wrong about him? Or maybe it was all an act to gain my trust?

I rose to my feet and followed him, not trusting what they would do with her. Before we could reenter the party, Zara cried out, "What about me? You can't just leave me here. Look what that scum did to me!"

Patrick paused but didn't even look back at Zara. Instead, he turned to one of the Fold members and murmured something I couldn't hear. The man nodded and then gestured to three others who closed in on Zara as she shouted and called me all manners of names.

What happened to her next I wouldn't know until morning. The only thing on my mind was Violet and this mysterious leader who I had hated from birth, but who I now find myself more intrigued by than anything in my life. Had this been what Asher had meant? Would befriending Patrick Blordril be the answers to all my prayers?

Only time would tell.

Chapter 14

I TRIED TO FOLLOW Patrick to the infirmary, but one of the other members, a man with black hair and odd reddish-brown eyes, stopped me.

"We will take it from here," he told me, his hands folded over in front of him, a no-nonsense look on his face.

"But she's my friend," I insisted.

The man frowned and then nodded toward my face. "Maybe you should worry more about yourself than your friend. It would be a pity if you scarred." The way he commented on my scarring was odd. He hadn't said it sarcastically, the way most would have. He seemed genuinely concerned I would ruin my face. Guess even the Crimson Fold cared about looks.

The reminder of the scratch on my face made me wince. I reached up to touch the swollen, tender skin, and it came back slightly bloodied. I sighed in defeat. "Where do I go?"

He gestured toward another part of the room where a man and woman sat filling out paperwork. "You can have one of the medics check you out."

One of medics probably heard him and rose to come toward me. He gestured for me to take a seat, his expression bored as though he saw situations like this all the time. His name-tag read 'Tomas' while his ID photo was one of equal disinterest.

He worked in silence, which was fine with me as I tried to listen to what was happening with Violet. They spoke in low murmurs, too soft for me to make out.

"Stay still," Tomas said when I leaned toward the curtained-off area.

I frowned and tried to obey as he cleaned off my scratches and placed some cool cream on them. Then he bandaged me up and stepped back. He didn't tell me to leave, just turned on his heel and went back to his desk.

"Uh ..." I sat on the table not sure if I should stay or go. When Tomas didn't turn around, and instead just stared down at his paperwork scribbling occasionally, I felt it safe to leave.

Sliding off the seat, I started toward Violet's bed, but when I came close, the same black-haired Fold member came into view. He shot me a warning look, and I changed my destination to the door. Giving one more concerned glance toward Violet, I headed out of the infirmary and started the walk back to my room.

No one waited for me at my room, and I stripped my clothes and climbed into bed. I lay there for a few moments before I remembered the makeup on my face and I got up and went to the bathroom to scrub it off.

Freshly scrubbed and more tired than I had ever been working a full day in the fields, I crawled under the covers. My mind whirled, today's events making my head hurt. Zara's attack hadn't been secret this time. Surely, she will be punished or better yet sent home, mind-wiped and tail between her legs.

My lips curled up at the thought. At least something good had come out of the scratches on my face. I only hoped Violet would be all right. Thinking of Violet made my smile to drop. I didn't understand why they wouldn't let me see her. It's not like I hadn't been there when she'd gotten hurt. Maybe they thought blood would make me sick? Or worse yet, they could be wiping her memory, however they did that, so she couldn't tell everyone about it. Which brought up another point: would they send her home? It was hardly fair to punish her for something that had been done to her, but it wouldn't be the first time someone blamed the victim.

The thoughts kept me up well into the night. It wasn't until the morning light began to filter through the curtains did I finally fall asleep. What felt like seconds later, someone banged on my bedroom door.

Groaning, I slid off the bed and grabbed the robe left for me off the back of a chair. I wrapped it around myself tying it tight as I approached the door. When I opened it, I expected to see Asher, or even the trio, there waiting to make me up for the last night of the Election but Venna stood there with a displeased look on her face.

"Can I help you?" I asked rubbing my eyes with a yawn.

"Oh dear, you look horrible," she cooed, placing a hand on my cheek. "They really should have had you stay in the infirmary with that other girl. Please tell me they gave you something for the pain."

I let her fuss over me for a moment before I pulled back and asked, "Didn't you come here for something?"

Her expression changed to a stony one, and she placed her hands in front of her. "I'm to escort you to Lord Beaford. He wishes to have a word with you."

When my face scrunched up in confusion, I winced. The scratches on my face still radiated pain even with after Tomas's treatment. The likelihood I wouldn't scar seemed like a daydream. I'd be happy if it didn't get infected.

"Give me a moment," I told her and then shut the door. I searched through the wardrobe for something I could wear. Luckily, I found a long shirt and a pair of pants shoved in the back of the wardrobe. Probably meant for sleeping in but I'd rather wear them than another frilly dress. I quickly dressed and found the boots I'd worn when I'd first arrived, shoved under my bed.

"Ready," I said as I opened the door.

Venna led me down the hallway, chitchatting about the gossip in the palace. "You know, everyone still thinks you are going to win the head spot. Even though that Violet girl is now number one."

"She is?" I asked surprised. I hadn't looked at the scoreboard this morning and, from the way my stomach growled, I'd slept straight through breakfast.

"Sure," Venna nodded. "But it's understandable after last night. That other girl, Zara, is it? She's a nasty piece of work. Shame on her parents." Her nose curled up in disgust.

I made a noise of agreement and then asked, "Do you know who is left? I didn't get a chance to look at the board this morning."

Venna smiled next to me. "Sure, three others were sent home though, but none of any importance, except that poor girl. Tillie, I think her name was. Four times she's been here, and they send her home again?"

Venna shook her head in displeasure. "They have surely given her brain damage from wiping her memory so many times."

"How do they do it?" I interrupted. "You know, wipe their memory? Is it a drug or some technology?"

The older woman quieted for a moment and then said, "I've never seen it myself. They always do it in secret, but I've heard rumors that it's some form of hypnosis. I wouldn't know more than that as I'm only a lowly servant." She said the last bit with a laugh.

"I don't think so," I argued. "Even as a servant, it must be better than being forced to dress up every day and be paraded around like a trophy which I'm sure is to be my fate."

"Hardly," Venna patted my hand, stopping us at a door. "You might be chosen for your looks, but you'll stay there because of your wit and your heart."

Frowning at her words, I didn't get the chance to ask what she meant before she knocked on the door and walked away. A voice from inside told me I could enter. I twisted the knob and peeked into the room. An office almost exactly like the one my father and I had argued in, but behind the desk sat Beaford.

When he saw me, he folded his hands over in front of him. "Please come in and shut the door behind you. We have much to discuss, you and I."

"We do?" I asked, coming before him and taking a seat on the opposite side of the desk. I didn't think there was anything I had to talk about with the short man. Even more so, the way he was looking at me so possessively made my skin crawl.

"Yes, we do," he answered and settled back into his seat. "I thought you might want to know your friend Violet is perfectly fine. A bit beat up, but she has been taken on as Maleria's companion and will have the best medics looking after her now."

"That's good to know, thank you." I didn't know who Maleria was, but I didn't doubt being a companion would provide Violet with more help than she could have gotten back home.

"Also, I'm not sure your relationship to the boy I've seen you hanging around with him as well as a few others, but Narq will be a servant in the palace from today on." He watched my face for a reaction, but I didn't really have one. Narq had helped me out, but that was about it. I didn't know him any better than I had known Violet though something in me had compelled me to rush to her aide when Zara had attacked.

When I didn't reply, Beaford's shoulders sagged a bit as if he'd expected me to cry out in objection. He fiddled with a letter opener on his desk, and I started to wonder what the real reason was for him calling for me.

"I'm sorry," he apologized, his eyes focused down on the desk. "This is a bit hard for me. I've never been good at making decisions. Your friend Tillie being here so many times can attest to that."

Any respect I had for Beaford, which was little, went down the drain. *He* had been the one to call Tillie back so many times? The one who had practically destroyed her mind, and any chance of her having a normal life? Just because he couldn't make up his mind? The sharpened letter opener in his hand suddenly seemed like it would look better in his eyeball.

"I called you here because I want to make an offer to you." His eyes met mine across the table, but I schooled my features not to show my rage. I'd make him pay for it later. When I sat by Patrick's side. Then all of them would pay.

"What is it?" I asked, my voice cool making him frown.

He soon got over it though and continued, "I know you are high up on the scoreboard and have no reason to think you won't be chosen as a convert, but I would like you to think of what that might really mean. If you chose to be my companion, you could have all the freedom in the world. Go where you like, do what you like, even wear what you like." He gestured to my outfit. "But if you become the convert of the leader of all of Alban, then you won't have those luxuries. You will be constantly watched, judged for your every action. Now, do you really want a life like that?" He questioned me as if it were not something I could ever want. "Someone like you could clearly see how such a position would be … unfitting."

I paused, trying to keep a hold of my emotions before I stood to my feet. "A person like me? You mean, someone from the Glade I take it?" I didn't wait for him to answer, my anger not letting me hold back any longer. "Maybe it is people like you who are the reason Alban needs a person like me. Someone who can't be bought, who has the welfare of the people, *all* the people, in mind, and not just those who live in the Inner Circle and Core."

"Now, see here—"

"No," I snapped, cutting him off, "*you* see here. I will win this, and I will become the next convert and have the ear of Patrick Blordril. If not because it is the right thing to do, then because of people like you and Zara who think I can't." I stomped from the room, letting the door slam behind me with a satisfying boom.

Chapter 15

BY TIME ASHER CAME to help me get ready, I was three plates of food into my angry eating. Back in the Glade, I couldn't have bouts like this. Food was scarce enough that eating it when you weren't hungry was unheard of.

But I wasn't in the Glade which was the problem.

Asher opened the door on his own when I didn't bother to get up to answer it. I barely glanced up from my plate of fluffy pastries to acknowledge him before I went back to shoving them in. Jelly from one of the pastries squirted out and dripped down my chin. I swiped at it with the back of my hand, causing Asher to flinch.

"Clarabelle," he said softly, taking the seat across from me. "I don't wish to alarm you, but it seems like you have been possessed." He waved a hand across the table and the pile of empty plates.

"I'm fine," I mumbled through bites.

"No, you're clearly not." He shook his head and then tried to take away the plate in front of me. My hand swiped out and snatched it back. I glared at him as I stuffed more dough into my mouth. I could feel the sugar rush hitting my head, and I didn't want to stop.

Asher frowned and leaned back in his seat, one leg crossed over the other. "This isn't like you. I've never seen you waste food like this. Nor would I expect it, given your upbringing."

"And that's the problem," I growled, swallowing the food in my mouth. "Everyone thinks they know what is best for me because I'm not like them. I'm from the Glade. I don't belong. I shouldn't even be here," I rambled on and then tossed the half-eaten pastry onto the table. "Well, I'll tell you what, I'm the only one who knows what I can and can't do. If I want to eat a million donuts, then I will. If I want to wear pants instead of your magnificent outfits, then I will. And if I want to be the convert for Patrick-flipping-Blordril, then I will be." I paused and took a few shallow breaths before swallowing a couple of times. The rich food I'd been downing swirled in my stomach like a tornado, threatening to come back up.

I jumped from the table my hand over my mouth and muttered, "I'm going to be sick."

Rushing to the bathroom, all the food I'd eaten came back up in burning clumps. A warm hand sat on my back, and another came around and held my hair away. A cool cloth was pressed against my neck, and Asher's voice murmured soothingly in my ear. "There's a girl. It's alright. You can be whatever you want to be. Just don't kill yourself with pastries. That'll just mean they all won."

Once I had emptied my stomach, I sat back and leaned against the tiled bathroom wall. "I know. Normally, I wouldn't even think of wasting so much food, even food from the Core, but he just made me so mad. I came back to my room and saw the tray of fruit and cheeses, and it made it even worse."

"Who made you mad?" Asher asked, stroking my forehead with the cloth.

"Beaford."

"Oh, that hack," Asher scoffed. "He's an old-fashioned fool, who wouldn't know an ascot from a handkerchief. I wouldn't take anything he says to heart."

I sighed and rubbed my eyes. "I didn't, not really anyway. But the way he kept telling me I'd be more suited as *his* companion compared to being in such an important position as a convert." I shook my head in disbelief. "I just couldn't take it anymore." I glanced over at Asher who watched me with a patient frown. "Did you know he's the one who kept having Tillie brought back?"

"Really?" Asher raised a brow. "I can't see that."

"Truly, he said so himself." I nodded. "Something about not being able to make up his mind. Or some bull."

Asher sat next to me on the floor, his eyes focused on something off in the distance. "At least, now she can never be invited again. She's over twenty-one now."

At his words, I sat up. "What's up with that, anyway? What does being over seventeen and under twenty-one have anything to do with being invited?"

My sponsor shrugged. "I suppose it's because that is the time in your life you are supposed to be searching for who you are. Where you belong. After twenty-one, you become harder to sway to their ways. But don't take my word for it." He smirked and caressed the side of my face. "I'm just the help."

I snorted and rose to my feet with him. "I doubt anyone would ever see you as just the help. You're too nosy."

"Too true," Asher responded with a smile. "But as it were, my nosiness is what is going to make you the new convert of Patrick-flipping-Blordril."

"How?"

"Well," Asher moved to the vanity, "First off, making sure you looked fabulous on all occasions was a must, but you also did a lot of the work for me."

"How so?" I cocked a brow at him. I didn't think I'd done anything except make myself look like an idiot, commit treason, and then get into a brawl. That didn't sound like the perfect candidate to me.

Asher gestured for me to sit down at the vanity and began to work on my hair. "If you had been prim and proper like the rest of those wretches that were invited, Patrick would have glanced your way no more than for a second."

"Not my fault you made the shoes miles high," I retorted and tried to turn and glare at him, but he forced me to sit forward.

"Then, your answers to the interview questions, I couldn't have been prouder to have you as my guest. Nothing that comes out of your mouth is fake or insincere. I bet they'd never expected someone like you to walk through their doors." He chuckled as he twisted my hair this way and that.

"I hadn't planned that either," I muttered.

"I know! Which is what made it so great."

"More like I'm lucky to have my head after yelling at them." I tried to slouch in my chair, but Asher tugged on my hair making me wince and sit up straight once more.

"Well, you have made more than your impression on our leader just from those two incidents but last night was the cherry on the top." He paused as he pinned my hair into an elaborate updo and slid a small tiara into place. Moving around to sit in the chair his companions usually used to do my makeup, he sat in front of me. "Why did you go to that girl's rescue? You barely know her."

The question shocked me. "Why wouldn't I?"

"That," Asher pointed a face brush at my face. "That right there is why you will make a difference in the Fold." He brushed the bristles across my face as he continued speaking. "You didn't have to help her, it wasn't like she was your best friend. In fact, most people would have let her get hurt simply because she was the competition."

"But that's not right." My mouth dropped open at his words. Would the rest of them really not have come to her aide simply because they wanted her out of the running?

"This may come to a shock to you, my dear Clarabelle," Asher said as he lined my lips. "But people are selfish. They don't go out of their way to help anyone, even a child. What you showed was compassion. Something this world deeply needs."

"Hmmm." I didn't know what to say to that. My father had raised me to care for everyone. As the overseer, one neighbor's problem was yours. You couldn't not get involved because it would be inconvenient for you. Then no one would get anywhere. I wanted to believe there were good people in the world and they weren't all like Asher described, but it was hard, even for me.

"There," Asher stated, getting to his feet and moving over to the bag he'd brought in with him when I was stuffing my face. The thought of food made my stomach roll. "Sadly, this will be my last outfit for you. Then you will go on to bigger and better places."

"But we'll see each other again, right?" My throat clogged at the thought of never seeing Asher again. He had been my one constant since I'd come here, and losing him and his gaggle of ladies seemed impossible.

"Of course," Asher said. "You think my girls and I would just abandon you?" He clicked his tongue as he shook his head.

I glanced around the room, not for the first time wondering where the others were. "Why didn't the others come?"

An emotion ran over Asher's face before he gave me a grim smile. "I made them stay behind this time, so I could have some alone time with you before the final event."

"Why?"

Instead, of answering me, Asher unzipped the last dress bag and revealed a large ball gown of shimmering crystal blue material. Each movement made the tiny gems on the skirt shine like diamonds. In awe, I walked toward it. I fingered the bodice, the material silky and smooth against my skin.

"Do you like it?" Asher eyed me, little lines on his face showing his apprehension.

"I love it," I said, beaming up at him. "It's your best by far."

Asher helped me into it, the material moving across my skin like a dream. I stared at myself in the mirror as he zipped up the back, still not quite believing I was wearing something so beautiful. If either of my stepsisters could see me now, they would die on the spot. They'd soon see it though, I had no doubt the cameras would be there tonight, and in this dress, there was little chance all eyes wouldn't be on me.

Suddenly, I couldn't wait for the ball.

181

Chapter 16

TEN LEFT. THERE WERE ten of us left whose fate had yet to be decided. By the end of the night, that would all change.

The final event would be held in a different part of the palace than the first two. There had been more of us then and with us now down to only a handful, there was no reason to compensate for the size.

When Asher brought me to the double doors, two servants were waiting on either side. They reached for the door handles, but Asher stopped them from opening them. He turned to me and took my hands, covered in long elbow-length gloves matching the amazing gown, in his.

"No matter what happens tonight, I want you to remember one thing."

"What's that?" I asked with a hint of a smile.

Asher leaned in and whispered in my ear, "You have the power to lift Alban back to greatness or burn it to the ground."

Shocked by his words, I pulled back. I didn't have a chance to ask him what he meant by it all before he turned on his heels and walked away, leaving me alone at the doorway to my fate.

The two servants opened the double doors, and I no longer had time to dwell on his words. I forced the shock from my face and hoped I gave a pleasant look as the cameras took me in. Ignoring them, I walked into the room which ended up being at the top of a large set of stairs. They led down into the room where the rest of the party was in full swing. There were fewer guests this time, but the ones who had been chosen as companions were there with their counterparts.

I searched the room for a familiar face but found none. Marsha hadn't been picked yet, so he had to be there somewhere. Tillie had been sent home, so I couldn't rely on her to be there to calm me with her dreamy way of speaking. Narq, though we weren't friends, had saved my life and would be better than nothing, but since he had been chosen as a servant, I doubted he'd be invited to the final party. As I descended the stairs, I wondered if Violet would attend, or if she would still be in the infirmary.

I thought of searching for her, but as I came down the stairs, all eyes turned to me. The room hushed as a figure stepped out of what seemed like nowhere and waited at the bottom of the steps.

Patrick.

Dressed in a tailored suit of white, with his hair and pale eyes, he would easily blend in with the walls had it not been for the blood red rose in his lapel. As it was, the sight of him made my stomach flutter. I still didn't know much about him, certainly nothing I didn't know already. Asher had thought we would make a good match so there must be something about him that I would like besides his good looks.

"Hello," I breathed out, my heart pounding in my ears as I stepped off the final stair.

Patrick smiled down at me his eyes crinkling at the sides. "You look lovely. Asher has outdone himself."

I blushed and dipped my head down. "He's really great."

"I would know." Patrick chuckled. "He's my cousin."

My head jerked up at his words. "What?"

The look on my face must have been more upset than I realized because Patrick quickly tried to explain. "A distant cousin. Not many people know. His request, not mine. Something about not wanting to be treated differently because of our relationship."

"I could see how that would bother him," I commented.

Asher didn't seem like the type to want to stand in anyone's shadow. With his wonderful creations, he wanted to be known for his talents and not have people like them simply because of who he was related to. I knew the feeling. All too often, I'd been given special treatment in school because of my father, which had made it even harder to make friends. Although, even if I had been able to, I wouldn't have hidden my father. I loved him too much.

"I have to say," I started after a moment, "I don't see the family resemblance." I walked deeper into the room forcing him to choose to follow me or not.

But he did, to my surprise.

"Well," he said from my side. "Like I said, it's a distant relationship. I'd be surprised if you guessed on your own."

"Still," I said, stopping at the refreshment table and picked up a glass of something bubbly, "he's so full of life and excitement while you ..." I trailed off and then clamped my mouth shut as I realized who I was talking to. I'd pretty much insulted the leader of all of Alban to his face, while we were on camera. If I didn't get kicked out for that, I'd have to be sure to watch myself in the future.

But I shouldn't have worried, Patrick threw his head back and laughed. A sound that drew the attention of many females, and even a few males. It was the kind of sound that swept through you and settled low inside making you feel warm and fuzzy.

"You are definitely something else, Clarabelle ... I mean, Clara." He caught himself at the last minute as he grinned down at me with a twinkle in his eye.

"So, I've been told," I muttered and buried my face in my glass. Maybe if I drank enough, I'd sound something more like a human being.

Patrick wasn't going to let me wallow though. He took the glass from my hand and sat it on the table and then offered me a hand. "Dance with me."

It was a command, not a question. One I wanted to obey, but before I could, an unpleasantly familiar face appeared next to us.

"Fancy meeting you here, Patrick," Zara cooed, completely ignoring my presence as she shoved her way between us.

I stared at the girl in utter revulsion, and any good feelings I had begun to harbor for our leader completely vanished. Without a word, I turned on my heel and pushed my way through the crowd. Rage boiled inside of me as I held my skirts in my hands, not caring who was watching. I didn't stop until someone caught me by the shoulders, pulling me to the side.

"Marsha." I almost sighed in relief when I saw his face.

"Where are you going in such a rush?" he asked smiling, but when his eyes focused on my face, his expression wilted. "What's wrong?"

"Nothing," I snapped, and then bit the inside of my cheek and changed my answer. "Everything."

Our eyes met the camera which had started to come our way. We couldn't talk freely here. Not without having it broadcasted across Alban or at least the Inner Circle.

"Here." Marsha took me by the hand and led me across the room and out a door.

Cool air touched my bare shoulders. We were outside, and it wasn't like the balcony in the other room. The door led to a part of the garden I hadn't had a chance to explore. Immediately I felt better than I had in days.

Marsha brought us over to a bench and sat me down. I tilted my head back and stared up at the dark sky, but just like in the Inner Circle there were too many lights to see any stars. Just one more thing they had taken away from me.

"Now," Marsha said, pulling my attention away from the sky. "What happened?"

My anger had lessened since we had come outside but it raged back up as I thought of Zara. "They let her stay."

"Who?"

"Zara," I snapped. "She already killed one of the guests and tried to kill me. Not to forget she had just beaten the crap out of Violet in front of everyone. But here she is." I jerked my hand toward the ballroom. "Walking around making people's lives miserable with no repercussions. Why?" I asked turning my gaze to Marsha. "Why would they let her stay?"

Marsha shrugged. "She's the mayor's daughter," he said as though it explained everything.

"So that gives her leave to commit murder?" I snarled. "She's not untouchable. Being the mayor's daughter doesn't mean that much, does it?"

"Maybe they thought it would look bad if they got rid of her? She has made things a bit livelier." I snorted, and he paused, shooting me a look. "Sure, the way she is going about it is completely wrong and messed up, but you have to think of it from their side. They sit up here in their palace, having little to do with us down below. This is the only time they can make a real impact on us. Maybe they planted Zara to create the extra conflict to show the rest of Alban that *they* aren't untouchable."

I blew out a harsh breath. "It's a shit way of showing it. Why make us all dress up just so they can slaughter us?"

Marsha patted me on the shoulder, "They're the Crimson Fold; it's what they do."

We were quiet for a few moments before Marsha spoke again. "You know what's funny?"

"What?" I glanced over at him, ready for anything to get my mind off what lay inside.

"That before this," - he gestured to the palace - "before we both got invited, I was working up the nerve to ask you out." He laughed bitterly before giving me a lopsided grin. "Looks like I've lost my chance."

I sat there, dumbfounded. Not that someone liked me, but that Marsha had actually thought he needed to work up the courage to ask me out. I wasn't desperate by any means. I mean, I didn't have a lot of guys beating down my door. None actually. But I'd thought I was more approachable than he was making me out to be. Plus, I'd always found Marsha attractive but not someone who would be interested in me, a girl from the Glade.

"You should have just asked," I said a moment later. "I would have said yes."

"Yeah?" His eyes locked with mine surprise on his face. "Well, then if we get out of this alive and not bound to anyone, I'll hold you to it."

"Count on it." I smiled and held his hand in mine, tightly.

Just then a throat cleared beside us. We turned at the same time to see Patrick Blordril standing with his hands behind his back and a frown on his face. Instantly, I dropped Marsha's hand. I didn't know why, but I felt guilty for talking about going out with him when I was supposed to be aiming to be Patrick's convert. Whatever that really entailed.

"I'll ... just let you two be alone," Marsha said, standing from the bench. He nodded to Patrick and gave me a meaningful look before heading back inside, leaving me alone with the leader of all of Alban.

Chapter 17

AWKWARDNESS FELL OVER US as I sat on the bench with Patrick standing beside me. Marsha had seemed more than eager to get out of there, which I couldn't blame him. I hardly knew what to say to normal people let alone the leader of all of Alban. Especially since we were sort of courting each other.

Would that be what it was called? I didn't think so. I'd been threatened to show up, or else my family gets shunned, and then paraded around like livestock for their pleasure. I couldn't count the number of times I'd been poked and prodded by Asher and his girls. Though, I could hardly blame them for any of it.

I could blame Patrick though.

"You're angry," he stated after a moment. He stayed standing but put his hands in his pockets, pushing the suit jacket back slightly to reveal the off-white shirt beneath. Even from here, I could see the outline of the muscles beneath. I'd never thought of him as a man, only as someone to focus all my problems on. It was a funny feeling.

"Yes," I answered, finally meeting his eyes with a fierce determination. Attractive or not, it didn't change the fact that he had done me wrong. Had done Violet and so many others wrong. I couldn't let my weakness distract me.

He watched me intently before saying, "It's because of that girl, correct? Zara?"

"Yes." Simple answers were the way to go when trying to hold my anger. I didn't want to blow my top now. There was too much at stake.

"I'm sorry if her presence upsets you," he said sincerely, and I believed him. "I don't agree with her being here."

"Then why is she?" I snapped and then caught myself before I could say any more.

Patrick winced. "I deserve your ire for certain, but I did try to have her removed. I was overruled."

I gaped at him. "You're the leader of Alban, the head of the Crimson Fold, and you were overruled? How does that even happen?"

Patrick sighed and then moved to sit next to me but paused. He seemed to be waiting for my permission which I reluctantly gave to him with a nod. Finally sitting down, he leaned forward, so his forearms lay against the top of his thighs. "I might be the leader, but I do have to answer to the other members. I don't have as much power as the people might believe."

"Then what's the point?" I asked without thinking. "Are you just a figurehead? A pretty face to put before the people to make them less likely to revolt against your deeds?"

Patrick turned his head toward me and smirked. "A pretty face, huh? I've never been called that."

I ducked my head in embarrassment. I hadn't meant to let his looks affect me so. Or to let on how I felt. Patrick Blordril was a mystery for sure. One I wished to figure out but not at the expense of my life. And I had little doubt Zara would take it if she could.

"Anyway," Patrick continued, bypassing my little comment, "when something like what happened with Zara occurs, we have to vote on what to do. I was one of the ones pushing for her removal. Especially after this." He reached up and touched the side of my face where the scratches had scabbed over, but even Asher's talented hands couldn't completely them cover up. "But too many of the others thought she was good for the audience. To see that even one of their own could turn on them in the right situation."

"So Marsha was right."

Patrick's brows raised at my comment. "Marsha? He's the boy who sat here before, correct?"

I nodded wishing I hadn't said anything. I didn't want Patrick to go out of his way to make sure Marsha was sent home. Or worse.

"Do you like this boy? Marsha?" he asked suddenly.

My mouth dropped open, and I struggled to find an answer. "He's my friend, so of course I like him."

Patrick gave me a look. "You know that's not what I meant. Do you care for him in a romantic manner?"

I turned my eyes away from him and stared up at the sky. I didn't want to lie but also wasn't sure how to answer him. I'd never really thought of Marsha that way until now.

"I could have," I said after a moment.

"What's stopping you?" He shifted closer to my side, pushing my large skirt into my thighs. "You could be with him now. No one is stopping you."

"But aren't they?" I half laughed, and the sound was not pleasant.

"If you could go home right now, would you?"

"Home is a relative question," I argued. "Back to the Inner Circle where I'm the strange girl who dresses funny and doesn't think like they do? Or back to the Glade where I'm the overseer's daughter who can't be trusted to be their friend, but I can stand by and watch them starve? Which one would you prefer me to go back to?"

"You can fix it."

Patrick's words startled me, almost giving me whiplash as I did a double take. Asher had practically said the same thing. I could fix it. All the wrong going on in Alban. I could make it better, make the Fold see the way things were set up was wrong, and here the very leader of them all sat saying the same thing.

"The system is broken. You and I both know this," Patrick explained. "Hell, even the other members of the Fold are aware of it, but it doesn't benefit them to fix it. Those who make the food and do the hard labor shouldn't be the ones who starve in the streets while those close to the Core throw up what they eat from overindulgence." The only thing that allowed me to believe his words was the utter disgust on his face.

"And I can fix this?" I asked, waiting for the other shoe to drop.

"Yes," he said, a bit excited as he grabbed my hands in his. "You could make all the difference. I knew the moment you stepped foot into the first impressions. You were the change we need."

I stared down at our hands, glad to have the gloves on to hide way my fingers were sweating. "Why can't you do it?"

"What?" He frowned at me.

"Why can't you tell them to change it? Why does it have to be? A know-nothing girl from the Glade." I shook my head and tried to take my hands back. "You're their leader, they should listen to you more than me."

"But I'm not you. It's hard to change a lifetime of thinking overnight. If I spoke up, they would revolt against me." Patrick held fast to my hands, drawing me closer until our faces were inches apart. His voice lowered as he spoke. "If I had you by my side, you could put those thoughts into their heads. At first, they would be tossed to the side as being new to our ways, but soon they will come to believe it too."

"How do you know?" I asked, mesmerized by the determination in his pale eyes.

"Because I have faith … in you," he murmured, stroking the side of my face. "All you have to do is say yes."

Before I knew what was happening, or could even block it, his mouth descended onto mine. It was the first kiss I'd ever experienced, and I didn't know how to react. At first, I sat frozen in place and then curiosity came over me. I pressed back, returning his kiss.

We stayed that way for a moment, his warm hand caressing the side of my face, our lips locked. It wasn't unpleasant, but I didn't feel a sudden rush of feeling like some girls talked about. I didn't want to marry this man or throw my whole life away. But I could sit there and let the leader of Alban kiss me for a few more moments.

Those moments were over too soon when a clock somewhere struck the hour. I jerked away from him, and a sharp pain hit my lower lip. I reached up to touch it, and blood came away. A growl sounded, and it took me a second before I realized it had come from Patrick.

My gaze locked onto him and what I saw caused me to jump to my feet. Brow furrowed, he had an intense look in his eyes, eyes that had changed from a lovely blue to a bright red. My heart pounded, and I took several steps back.

The movement caused Patrick to seem to remember himself and his eyes changed back. He stood to his feet, a hand reached out to me, but I shook my head and stepped out of his reach.

"Please, Clara. Let me explain." His pleas were too late because I'd already turned on my heels and ran back to the palace.

Chapter 18

PULLING THE DOORS TO the ballroom open, I threw myself inside. The room turned at my entrance the camera zooming in on me. I held my hand up to hide my face as I pushed my way through the crowd.

I could hear Marsha calling out my name, but I ignored him. The only thing on my mind was getting as far away from Patrick Blordril and the rest of these monsters.

Getting up the stairs in my long dress proved to be harder than when I had entered. I hadn't been in a rush to get away then though. I kept tripping over my skirt and knew I'd torn it in some places from my careless steps. I grabbed the full part of the skirt and held it to me as I ran up the stairs.

The doors didn't open for me this time. I had to tug the large door open myself, but once it shut behind me, relief didn't come. My feet kept moving me further and further away from the music, the laughter, the prying eyes.

Eyes. Red eyes. The feral look on Patrick's face came back to my mind, and my feet moved even quicker.

I didn't know where I was going, only that I needed to get away. I couldn't go back to my room; if Patrick came looking for me, that would be the first place he'd look. I thought briefly to search for Asher but then he was Patrick's cousin, he must know what they are, and he'd kept it from me.

I found a large set of double-doubles, the sign above it said, *Library.* It was a good a place as any to hide. I had said in my interview I didn't read so maybe they wouldn't look for me here.

Once inside, I found myself alone. I found a chair and collapsed in it. I didn't cry or scream, no theatrics from this girl, but I did take in large gulps of air as I tried to come to terms with what happened. My mind reeled with confusion and horror.

What were they? I'd never seen anyone look like that. Were they sick? I'd never heard of anything like them. Then a thought came to me. It might not be all of them, it could just be Patrick. If it was, then the Fold has been hiding a big secret from the rest of us. But if it turned out to be all of them, then they needed to be outed. The people deserved to know who was ruling them.

But would anyone believe me without proof? I didn't have anything but my word against theirs, and they could say I was out of my mind. Seeing things. Then I'd be put away where I couldn't tell anyone or worse yet have my memory wiped.

No, I couldn't go public until I knew what I was up against and could prove it. Then I remembered I was in a library. Getting to my feet, I rushed to the shelves. Surely, there had to be something here about them. Something to help me prove my case.

At first, I didn't find anything. The majority of the books were stories or books about numbers and history. I knew some of our history. There used to be lots of cars and large buildings, more people than we had now. So many that the world became overpopulated. Then an epidemic had hit, and barely anyone survived. Alban rose up from the ashes of what was left, in some place they had called Alabama. I was sure it was why we called our little country that, to honor where we came from.

The history that had been passed down to us was a watered-down version we all just accepted because we didn't know any better. Too worried about surviving to care about how we got there. But I'd been wrong. I should have been worried, asked questions. Because if our leaders were monsters then there was a reason they were at the top and we at the bottom, barely scraping by.

After what seemed like hours of searching, I finally found something. A book with a leather cover, a bit beat up but with the title still legible.

"A Guide for the Newly Converted," I read aloud. Moving over to a chair, I opened the book carefully, afraid it would fall to pieces in my hands. I stared at the words searching for something that could help me. Anything.

The first few chapters were about the election. How the person should be tested before electing them for conversion. Then there were warnings about picking someone based solely on looks, or one of too strong a mind.

"They'd screwed up there," I scoffed to no one.

I continued to read until I came to a part about marking the elected. "On the night of the election, one must draw the blood of the one they wish to convert to make the claim official," I read aloud. "This will mark them as yours and keep any other potential members of the nest at bay."

Nest? What the hell are they talking about? We weren't birds. The marking worried me. No one, not Asher or Daphne had mentioned anything about being marked.

My finger touched my lip where it had already begun to scab over. I didn't doubt that it had been Patrick's way of claiming me, though I had been the one to jerk away. If I hadn't done it, would he have found another way? I didn't like to think so.

I turned my attention back to the book. It went on to explain the ritual of changing over a convert. Some fancy words would be spoken, I'd have to promise to be part of their nest, and then the last part made my stomach coil into a tight knot. The marking was not the last time I'd have to have my blood drawn. It would be part of the ceremony as well.

"The blood of the convert must be drained until the heart slows," I said my heart beating harder, panic setting in with each word I read. "It is important to get the moment right or else the convert will be lost. Then, when the time is right, the convert must drink from the master."

Master. Patrick.

The thought of drinking anyone's blood made me sick to my stomach. I decided then and there that I wouldn't be drinking anyone's blood. They'd have to kill me first.

I came to the end of the chapter as it described what would happen to the convert after the exchange. Three words stood out for me. Hunger. Immortal. Vampire.

As I tried to process these words, the door to the library swung open. I dropped the book to the floor as I stood to my feet. Marsha stumbled in, holding his neck with his hand. He had a small smile on his face as if he'd drunk too much wine.

"There you are," he giggled. I rushed to his side as he tripped over his feet and almost fell to the ground.

"Marsha," I held onto him though his weight pulled me down, "What happened?" I tried to move his hand to see, but he pushed me away.

"I think someone spiked my drink," he laughed and turned about the room. "I was talking to one of the members, Tris, I think is her name."

"Marsha," I tried again, grabbing at his shoulders. "You should sit down before you hurt yourself."

"Oh," he chuckled, "I already did that." He finally sat down, letting me see his neck. "Like, I said, I was talking to Tris, and we were having a great time. Someone yelled out to me and then I must have tripped or something because suddenly I was on the floor and my neck was bleeding."

I saw now what he talked about. A small cut, not much bigger than the one on my lip lay across his neck. It still bled slightly if prodded at, but it wasn't too deep. Relief fell over me as I realized he'd be okay but then just as fast, realization settled in.

Tris, a short, plump woman with dark multi-toned hair and bright green eyes, had been the other one who would pick a convert. The wound on Marsha's neck wasn't just from an accident. No, it would be too much of a coincidence. She must have done it to him as her way of marking him.

"Marsha," I said, a seriousness in my tone. "We have to get out of here."

"What?" Marsha looked up at me, his eyes dopey. "Why? Aren't you having fun?"

"No, I'm not." I shook my head. "And neither are you. We're in danger."

"You don't know what you are talking about." Marsha shook his head and then smiled. "I know what we can do. Let's go on that date we talked about. Right now." He stood to his feet, a bit wobbly, but he stayed upright. "We can go raid the kitchen and then eat while we watch the stars. Doesn't that sound like fun?"

"Yes," I answered, trying to keep him with me. "But wouldn't that be more fun back home? In the Inner Circle?"

It was on the tip of my tongue to tell him what I'd found out, but it was too bizarre even for me. There was no such thing as vampires. They were just something people made up to scare little kids. Besides, the ones I'd heard about couldn't stand the daylight, and I'd seen Patrick in the sun.

Hadn't I?

I suddenly couldn't remember a time I'd seen him outside when it wasn't dark. We'd done the initial interviews and such inside, and the curtains had been drawn then. The parties themselves were at night, with no chance of being hit by the sun.

The more I tried to rationalize it the more it started to make sense. The man I'd been talking to, the one whose attention I'd been vying for, wasn't human at all. Not really. If the stories were true, he was little more than the walking dead, and he wanted to make me one of them.

Over my dead body. Which sadly might actually be the case.

Chapter 19

I HELPED MARSHA BACK to his room because he couldn't be trusted to walk a straight line let alone find his way on his own. He still wasn't acting like himself, and I hoped it was because of alcohol and not whatever Tris had done to him.

After Marsha passed out in his room, I started the long trek back to mine. I hadn't told him what I found out. Not only because he wasn't coherent enough to listen but because I didn't know if he would believe me. Hell, I didn't believe it even though I'd read it myself.

I had the book from the library tucked under my arm. I wasn't about to let it out of my sight anytime soon. Plus, there had to be more information in there I could use to get out of this marking thing ... if what Patrick had done had been marking me.

I half expected Patrick to be waiting for me in my bedroom but to my surprise, it was Asher who stood at my door. I slowly approached him, hoping he wouldn't see where I had accidentally torn the hem of his beautiful dress. I moved the book into my hand, hiding it inside the full skirt, but he wasn't paying any mind to it.

"Clara." He sighed, relief on his face. "I heard you ran out of the party. Again." He gave me a chastising look before adding, "I thought maybe something had happened."

"What?" I cocked my hip to the side and glared at him. "Like finding out you're Patrick's cousin? Or that he's a vampire?"

Asher's eyes widened and then darted around the hallway. When no one came running or whatever is it that he'd expected to happen, he ushered me into my room. I tried to talk again, but he pressed his finger to his lips in a shushing motion. Leaving me standing in the middle of the room he darted around, checking light shades and even the mirror before turning back to me.

"Sorry, but I had to be sure they hadn't put monitors in your room."

"Monitors?" I asked, glancing around for whatever he was talking about.

"Recording devices. Sometimes if they think someone isn't trustworthy, even a guest, they'll put them around their bedroom to find out what they are thinking. Luckily, I think you are good," Asher said, but the look on his face wasn't relief. It was worry.

"Okay, so what now?" I sighed, sitting down on the edge of my bed. I made sure to tuck the book under me, so he couldn't see it. I'd trusted Asher up until this point, but after everything I'd learned tonight, I wasn't sure that was still a good idea.

"You tell me everything," Asher said, sitting by my side.

So, I did. I told him about Patrick showing up at the bottom of the stairs. How he had told me they were cousins and then how Zara had shown up to ruin it all. I skipped the bit with Marsha and me. That was private and not relevant at all to what I wanted to know. The conversation between Patrick and I was a bit trickier because it all jumbled together under the pressure of hormones. I did get across a clear picture of what Patrick looked like after I'd nicked myself on his teeth, which I explained fully.

"And that's all?" Asher asked, prodding for more information as if he knew I was keeping something back.

"That's it," I promised as I sat harder on the book beneath me.

Asher kept quiet for a few moments before he asked, "What makes you think he's a vampire then, and not just an aggressive kisser? There are plenty of people who love a good nibble every once in a while."

I flushed and stared down at the ground. Talking about people's preferences wasn't something I was used to and doing so with Asher made it even worse. Finally, when I could look him in the eye again, I said, "I'm not stupid, Asher."

"I never said you were," he said, patting my hand as if I were a child. That pissed me off. "But you can't jump to conclusions like that, not here. You walk a fine line as it is and if we want you to be chosen then—"

"But I have been!" I jumped to my feet, forgetting for a moment that the book was under me. It slid to the ground with a loud thump, but before I could reach for it, Asher scooped it up.

"What's this?" His eyes widened as they landed on the title, and then he thumbed through it with an increasing amount of shock.

"See?" I said, coming up close to him, "I know all about the converts. It says it right there in the book. He marked me, and I think Tris marked Marsha." I left out the bit that she had also slipped him something. I'd figure out what to do about that later.

"That liar," Asher growled, clutching the book in his hand.

"Okay, not the reaction I expected but better than nothing." I reached for the book, but Asher jerked it out of the way. "Hey, give it back. You know what I said was true. That's mine. I'm going to need it if I'm going to get out of this mess."

Asher threw his hands up in the air with a dramatic cry. "Fine, you're right. Patrick's a vampire. The whole stinking Crimson Fold are vampires. For crying out loud, I'm one!"

I gaped at Asher admission and took a few steps back from him. My movement caused him to drop his arms and frown.

"Don't look at me like that," he almost whimpered. "I'm not going to hurt you. Besides, you're not my type." He smirked, and for a second, I almost believed him.

And then the anger came. "You knew this whole time and didn't say anything?" I pointed a finger at him, my voice rising with each word.

"Don't look at me. It wasn't my idea to lie about what we are. It's theirs." He gestured wildly with the book. "They're all about secrecy to the point where they will convert someone and tell them there is no guide to help you with the transition. Blasted liars." He scowled down at the book.

The reality of what was happening started to set in and I sank down to the floor. "So," I said, my voice small, "how long have you been a vampire?"

Asher sat down next to me, letting his long legs stretch out before him. "Only about a century or two. That's why Patrick and I are only distant cousins. He's almost eight hundred years old."

"Eight hundred?" I gaped at him. "What the crap! And I'm supposed to marry this guy?"

Asher gave me a pointed look. "Marry is a bit childish. Being a convert is forever. Literally. If you'd been a companion, then you might have been married."

"Ah ha!" I wagged a finger at him. "I knew your companions weren't just your helpers."

The sponsor had the decency to blush. Could vampires even blush? Either way, his face did look like it had blood running through it. I put the thought away for another time. The mechanics of their physiology was too much for me to handle right then.

"My girls are my companions, yes, but I haven't lain with any of them. We aren't married, nor will we ever be." The way he explained it held a hint of sadness to it, and I wished he'd tell me more. But I didn't dare to ask.

"So, is there any way out of this?" I asked, bumping my hand against the book.

"Not that I know of." He sighed and leaned back against the bed. "Take heart in knowing they won't convert you right away. There is a whole process. Your family must get used to being without you, so they don't start to ask questions. Then there's the whole re-education process where they are supposed to start making you think you want to be converted."

"But I already know about it."

"Ah, but they don't know that. They will flower you with gifts and praises, making you think you are welcome in their world so that you will do anything they ask of you. Then," - he held his finger up with a sense of finality - "then you will be turned before you even realize it is happening."

I snorted. "That seems hard to believe. I think I would notice all my blood being drained from me."

"You'd be surprised," Asher muttered. "Though some make their converts so in love with them, they want nothing else than to be with them forever. Which I feel is what Patrick would have done with you had you not figured it out."

"I don't believe in love," I stated, wrapping my arms around my legs. "There's love for a family member, a child, but not for each other. No one cares that much and those who do always want something."

"What a sad existence that must be." Asher made a small sound in his throat, as though he might cry before his hand stroked my tousled hair. I forced myself not to flinch at his touch, reminding myself he had done so more intimately during the last few days.

My existence might be sad to Asher, but it had kept me alive. I had loved my mother very much, but she'd died leaving a huge hole in me. I loved my father as well, but I knew eventually he too would die. If I became immortal, a vampire, then everyone I know, anyone I'd ever care about, would eventually die. No. Loving someone would never be in my cards. Not in this lifetime.

Chapter 20

IT WAS THE FINAL morning, the last day I would see the scoreboard in my room before they moved me to another suite. At least, that was what Asher told me.

There would be an announcement ceremony where everyone would come together and congratulate me on my position. While that was happening, all my belongings would be moved to a new room, one close to Patrick. Asher said that after a few days, I'd be allowed to go back to the Inner Circle to get any sentimental belongs, but for the most part, everything would be provided for me.

Since it was my last day, I didn't rush to get up. I lay there in my bed, staring up at the ceiling. Maybe if I stayed there, they'd forget about me.

Just as I had the thought, a knock sounded on my door. Before I could tell them to go away, a white head of hair peeked in. Venna.

"Hello, dear." She smiled at me as she pushed the door open with her hip. Carrying a tray through the doorway, she entered but didn't place it on the table the way all the others had. Instead, she brought it to me in bed. I sat up on the array of pillows and let her prop the tray on my lap.

"Thank you," I said, looking down at the delicious food. There were fruits and cheeses as usual but also large fluffy cakes and sausage. After yesterday the very sight of it made me sick to my stomach.

The disgust I felt must have shown on my face because Venna sat beside me with a worried look. "Do you not like it? I could go get something else."

She stood to leave, but I stopped her with my hand. "No, this is fine. Just not in the food kind of mood."

She gave me a small, understanding smile. "I understand. I'd be overwhelmed in your position as well. You've got the highest position there is! It's all anyone could talk about."

Great, I said to myself but then smiled at her. "Yes, exactly. Just nervous."

"Well, don't be." She patted me on the arm and then moved over to the screen when it turned on while we were talking. "You were a shoe-in to begin with, besides all the mishaps that occurred." She made a displeased noise as she stared at the screen.

"What is it?" I asked from my place in bed. Though I wasn't hungry, I picked up a piece of sausage and bit into it. The juices filled my mouth, and suddenly I became ravenous.

"See, you just needed to get started," Venna said and then frowned. "I'm surprised that Zara girl wasn't one of the two who were sent home."

"She wasn't?" I asked, almost choking on my food. I coughed and hit my chest to get the piece out.

"Sadly, no." Venna shook her head. "She's going to be Beaford's companion."

Beaford. The very sound of his name made my fist close around the bread in my hand, crumbling it to pieces. I should have known he would choose her.

To Venna, I said, "I'm sure they will be very happy together." In a shallow grave, I added silently.

Venna gave a curt nod. "At least, your friend Violet got a good one. Maleria has always been one of my favorite of the fold. She's very kind to the staff and has the most beautiful singing voice."

I still hadn't met Maleria but took Venna's word for it. I suddenly wanted to ask her if she knew they were all vampires, but I refrained. If they all knew, then it would hardly be a secret. It would be leaked to the rest of Alban within hours.

So, instead of asking what I really wanted, I asked, "What about Marsha?"

"Oh," she smiled slyly. "He's as lucky as you and got his own member to convert for."

I knew it. The nick on his neck had been Tris marking him. So much for the he-had-an-accident theory. Unfortunately, he didn't know anything about marking, or what we were in for. I had to find time to get him alone, so I could fill him in. Maybe if there were two of us, we'd have more of a chance to get out of here. Though, the way he had acted last night didn't give me high hopes. Marsha seemed to take everything at face value and would no doubt think their gifts and praises were their way of showing him kindness.

I wasn't so fooled.

With a newfound determination, I moved the tray out of my lap and jumped from the bed. I found the outfit Asher had laid out for me to wear today. Thankfully, no dresses lay beneath. Instead, I found a dark charcoal pantsuit with a red shirt beneath. A pair of half-inch wedges sat below that I slipped into after I dressed. I let my hair roll freely down my back, the updo from last night causing it to fall in waves.

I'd washed all the makeup off my face before going to bed, but Asher had left me specific instructions on how to apply what he had left for me. A bright red lipstick to match the shirt and a pale eyeshadow for my eyes. I tried to line my lids but failed so many times I about gave up before Venna came to the rescue.

"I used to do my sister's makeup all the time back in the Inner Circle," she commented as she applied the pen to my eyelids.

"What happened to her?" I asked, suddenly wanting to know more about her.

"Oh," she sighed, "she's still there. She sends me cards and pictures of her children. I go visit once every few years, but it's hard to get away, you know?" She smiled at me, a sad sort of smile, so I simply nodded.

"There, you're ready." Venna stepped back and let me look at myself.

Compared to all the other nights, this time I looked more like me. A fierce and determined me, but me nonetheless. At least I wouldn't be going into this pretending to be someone I'm not.

"Thank you." I hugged her briefly. She giggled, then squeezed me back.

When we were finished, Venna led me down a hallway and toward the room we'd had our interviews in. People were already piled in the doors, chatting away excitedly. I searched for Marsha but couldn't find him. Violet stood next to the Fold member she'd be companion too. Maleria. Long hair that reached her backside, she wore a dress that seemed to float around her. Those around her seemed happy which gave me hope that Violet would be okay.

Now, if only I would be.

I started to move through the room, determined to find Marsha and explain to him what was going on, but someone caught me by the elbow. Turning around, I froze in place at the sight of Patrick holding me. I swallowed hard and pushed down the fear that told me to run.

He smiled down at me, but even *I* could see it was fake. Then without warning, he brought me into his arms. He smelled of flowers and sandalwood, a heady smell that tickled my nose.

"Please, don't scream," he whispered in my ear. "I will explain everything after, but for now we have to put on a show for them. Make them see we are the happy couple they all think we are. Remember, you have the power to make a difference."

"I won't be turned into a vampire," I blurted out a bit louder than I meant, causing a few people to look our way. At least the cameras were too busy focusing on the others to notice us yet.

"And you won't." He clutched me tighter. "Not unless you want to, but it is very important that we keep up pretenses. Understood?"

I nodded against his chest and then, almost as suddenly, he let me go. Before any other words could be said he directed us to a small podium. He stood behind it with me at his side, my hand held in his.

"Thank you for all coming to this momentous occasion," he said into the microphone causing a round of applause and cheers to sound. "This has been our most fruitful Election yet, and I think I speak for everyone when I say that it will be one I remember for years to come." His eyes moved to me at that moment. To others, it might have been a look of love and adoration, but I knew it for what it was.

A warning. Don't screw this up or they'll kill us both.

I beamed back at him, which seemed to satisfy the crowd as they cooed. Patrick turned from me and went on to speak about tradition and the example we must set for the people. The words pouring out of his mouth spoke of things I had little doubt the Crimson Fold knew anything about. Or ever would.

They might think they were all powerful, but I knew better. Even their own leader wanted to put them down a peg. The problem was, how far was he willing to go? How much of this would be of my own free will and how much of it be me being moved like a chess-piece in his long-standing game?

I stood there with my hand clutched in his, a fake smile on my face, with one thought in my mind.

When the time came, would he ever let me go?

About the Author

Erin Bedford is an otaku, recovering coffee addict, and Legend of Zelda fanatic. Her brain is so full of stories that need to be told that she must get them out or explode into a million screaming chibis. Obsessed with fairy tales and bad boys, she hasn't found a story she can't twist to match her deviant mind full of innuendos, snarky humor, and dream guys.

On the outside, she's a work from home mom and bookbinger. One the inside, she's a thirteen-year-old boy screaming to get out and tell you the pervy joke they found online. As an ex-computer programmer, she dreams of one day combining her love for writing and college credits to make the ultimate video game!

Until then, when she's not writing, Erin is devouring as many books as possible on her quest to have the biggest book gut of all time. She's written over thirty books, ranging from paranormal romance, urban fantasy, and even scifi romance.

Come chat me up!
www.erinbedford.com
Facebook.com/erinrbedford
twitter.com/erin_bedford
Don't forget to follow me on Goodreads, Pinterest, Instagram, and YouTube!

Want to be the first to know about my new releases?
Erinbedford.com/newsletter

www.ingramcontent.com/pod-product-compliance
Lightning Source LLC
Chambersburg PA
CBHW070937190726
48292CB00004B/1220